Praise for the
Chocoholic Mysteries

The Chocolate Bear Burglary

"Do not read *The Chocolate Bear Burglary* on an empty stomach because the luscious . . . descriptions of exotic chocolate will have you running out to buy gourmet sweets . . . a delectable treat." —*Midwest Book Review*

"[Carl] teases with descriptions of mouthwatering bonbons and truffles while she drops clues. . . . [Lee is] vulnerable and real, endearingly defective. . . . Fast-paced and sprinkled with humor. Strongly recommended." —*I Love a Mystery*

"Kept me entertained to the very last word! . . . A great new sleuth . . . interesting facts about chocolate . . . a delicious new series." —*Romantic Times*

The Chocolate Cat Caper

"A mouthwatering debut and a delicious new series! Feisty young heroine Lee McKinney is a delight in this chocolate treat. A real page-turner, and I got chocolate on every one! I can't wait for the next." —*Tamar Myers*

"As delectable as a rich chocolate truffle, and the mystery filling satisfies to the last prized morsel. Lee McKinney sells chocolates and solves crimes with panache and good humor. More, please. And I'll take one of those dark chocolate oval bonbons. . . ." —*Carolyn Hart*

"One will gain weight just from reading [this] . . . delicious. . . . The beginning of what looks like a terrific new cozy series." —*Midwest Book Review*

"Enjoyable . . . entertaining . . . a fast-paced whodunit with lots of suspects and plenty of surprises . . . satisfies a passion for anything chocolate. In the fine tradition of Diane Mott Davidson." —*The Commercial Record*

Also by JoAnna Carl

The Chocolate Cat Caper
The Chocolate Bear Burglary

The Chocolate Frog Frame-Up

A Chocoholic Mystery

JoAnna Carl

A SIGNET BOOK

SIGNET
Published by New American Library, a division of
Penguin Group (USA) Inc., 375 Hudson Street,
New York, New York 10014, U.S.A.
Penguin Books Ltd, 80 Strand,
London WC2R 0RL, England
Penguin Books Australia Ltd, 250 Camberwell Road,
Camberwell, Victoria 3124, Australia
Penguin Books Canada Ltd, 10 Alcorn Avenue,
Toronto, Ontario, Canada M4V 3B2
Penguin Books (N.Z.) Ltd, Cnr Rosedale and Airborne Roads,
Albany, Auckland 1310, New Zealand

Penguin Books Ltd, Registered Offices:
80 Strand, London WC2R 0RL, England

First published by Signet, an imprint of New American Library,
a division of Penguin Group (USA) Inc.

First Printing, December 2003
10 9 8 7 6 5 4 3 2 1

PUBLISHER'S NOTE
This is a work of fiction. Names, characters, places, and incidents either are
the product of the author's imagination or are used fictitiously, and any resemblance to actual persons, living or dead, business establishments, events, or
locales is entirely coincidental.

For Dave,
a good guy to have around

Acknowledgments

As usual, I borrowed expertise from many of my friends to write this book. Of particular help were the experts at Morgen Chocolate, Dallas, including Betsy Peters, Rex Morgan, and Andrea Pedraza; Tom Bolhuis, expert on wooden boat restoration; Dick Trull and Judy and Phil Hallisy, experienced sailors; Anne and Chuck Wingard and their 1928 Chris-Craft Cadet; lawman Jim Avance, and great friends and neighbors Doyle Bell, Susan McDermott, and Tracy Paquin. Information on historic preservation and related legal issues came from Janet Schmidt, chair of the Historic District Commission of Saugatuck, Michigan; Ellen Clark, Saugatuck City Clerk; and from *Building the New and Rehabilitating the Old: A Builder's and Owner's Guide*, published by the Saugatuck-Douglas Historical Society. Historical information on chocolate was cribbed from *The True History of Chocolate* by Sophie D. Coe and Michael D. Coe.

Chapter 1

If you're going to have a fistfight in a small town—and avoid a lot of talk about it—the post office is not a good place for the battle.

And shortly before five o'clock in the afternoon—when it seems every merchant in town is dropping off the mail and lots of the tourists are buying stamps—is not a good time for it.

The fight between Joe Woodyard and Hershel Perkins erupted in the Warner Pier Post Office at 4:32 on a Monday afternoon in late June. Later I decided that it had been planned that way. And I didn't think Joe was in on the plan.

I was one of the local merchants who witnessed the fight, since I walked into the post office with a handful of outgoing statements for TenHuis Chocolade just in time to hear Joe speak.

He sounded calm. "What are you talking about, Hershel?"

Hershel Perkins did not sound calm. He was almost shouting. "It's about the old Root Beer Barrel. Don't try to act innocent!"

"The old drive-in? I'm trying to sell it."

"Yes, you money-grubbing piece of . . ."

Those were fighting words to Joe, I knew, because Joe—who happens to be my boyfriend—was in a financial hole right at the moment. It's a long story, but he needed money, even if he had to grub for it, and the sale of the dilapidated and abandoned drive-in restaurant might be the raft that kept his business afloat.

Joe raised his voice just a little when he answered. "What is your interest in this, Hershel?"

"I hear you might tear it down!"

"Tear it down? It's already fallen down."

"It's a piece of history!"

"History?" Joe sounded puzzled, as well as annoyed. "It's a bunch of boards lying in a parking lot. It's junk."

I was all the way inside the post office now, and I could see Hershel. He seemed to be puffing himself up. Not that Hershel was all that small. He was at least five nine, just a few inches shorter than I am. He was around forty, with a broad face and a wide, narrow-lipped mouth that made him look like a frog. It was a resemblance he seemed to relish—he combed his thin hair flat and always wore green shirts, flannel in winter and cotton in summer. Even his voice was a froglike croak, and he went places in a green canoe named the *Toadfrog*.

He gave an angry grunt. "Junk! You call it junk? It's vernacular architecture!"

Joe laughed.

Hershel went nuts. He rasped out incoherent phrases. Words like "typical commercial," "innovation," "rehabilitation," "social geography," and "culturally significant." None of it made sense to me—and I was willing to bet it didn't make sense to Hershel, either. Hershel is not one of the brightest bulbs shining on Warner Pier, Michigan.

Joe tried to talk over the ranting, which meant he had to raise his voice. "Hershel, I already talked to the Planning Department. The Historic District Commission has no interest in that property since the building was destroyed by an act of God."

Hershel kept up the angry bullfrog act, although hollering out "architectural ethnicity!" is not an effective way to argue.

Finally Joe did absolutely the worst thing he could have done—even worse than laughing. He turned his back on Hershel and reached for his post office box.

Hershel gave a loud roar and began to pummel Joe's shoulders with both fists.

Joe whirled around, throwing up his elbows to protect his face. Then he caught hold of Hershel's arms—first the left and then the right—and he whirled again. He pinned Hershel against the wall of post office boxes, almost the way he had pinned his opponents to the mat in the days when he was a high school wrestling champ.

Hershel finally shut up.

"Hershel," Joe said very quietly, "you can't go around hitting people. Get in your canoe and paddle home."

A couple of Warner Pier locals—one of them Hershel's brother-in-law, Frank Waterloo—appeared beside Joe. From the back of the room I heard another deep voice, this one smooth and slightly accented with Spanish. It was our mayor, Mike Herrera. "Yes, Hershel," he said, "pleeze go home. We have a forum for discussion of theese design matters. You can bring it up at the Preservation Commission. There ees no need to battle it out here. Not weeth all our summer visitors as sweetnesses."

The altercation had upset Mike. I could tell by his long "E's." Mike was born in Texas, and his accent usually tends more toward a Southwestern drawl than Spanglish.

Frank Waterloo, who's a bald, hulking guy, made his voice soft and gentle as he spoke to his brother-in-law. "Let's go, Hershel," he said.

Joe let go of Hershel. Hershel eyed the ring of guys around him. I swear he flicked his tongue in and out like a frog after flies. Then he walked slowly toward the street door, ignoring Frank. After Hershel pulled the door open, he paused and looked back. "That's what you say!" he said hoarsely.

He went outside, followed by Frank, then poked his head back in for a final croak. "I'll file charges!"

And he was gone. Nervous laughter swept the post office, and a couple of guys went over to Joe and assured him they'd back him up if Hershel filed any kind of complaint.

"The guy's crazy," Trey Corbett said. "The Historic District Commission has no interest in seeing the Root Beer Barrel rebuilt." Trey is a member of the commission.

"You haven't voted yet," Joe said.

Trey ran a hand over his thin, wispy hair and adjusted his thick glasses. To me Trey looks like a middle-aged boy. He's only in his mid-thirties, but his worried expression and nerdy appearance make him look as if he ought to be older. He doesn't sport a pocket protector, but he looks as if he should.

Trey shook his head. "Besides, Hershel hit you first. You only punched him in self-defense."

"Joe didn't punch him at all," I said. "He just griped—I mean 'grabbed'! He grabbed him." No harm in getting that idea foremost in the public mind right away.

Mike Herrera said, "Joe, you handled it as well as you could. But we sure doan want any gossip right at this point, do we?"

I wondered what that meant, but I decided this wasn't a good time to ask. So I spoke to Joe. "Are you hurt?"

Joe shook his head. "I'm fine, Lee." He turned to Mike and Trey. "Let's forget it. Hershel's just a harmless crank."

"He's a crank," Trey said. "But that doesn't mean he's harmless. Some cranks wind up walking up and down the streets with an Uzi."

"I'm no mental health expert," Joe said. "See you later." He turned to me. "You going back to the shop?"

"Oh, yeah. I'm there till closing."

"I'll walk down with you."

I dumped my invoices into the proper slot while Joe closed his post office box and stuck his mail in his shirt pocket. We walked down Pear Avenue toward TenHuis Chocolade. TenHuis—it rhymes with "ice"—is where my aunt, Nettie TenHuis, makes the finest European-style luxury bonbons, truffles, and molded chocolate in the world and where I'd be on duty until after nine o'clock.

The Fourth of July, when the biggest invasion of tourists hits the beaches of Lake Michigan, was still more than a week away, but the sidewalks of Warner Pier were crowded, and cars, vans, and SUVs were parked bumper to bumper. The three classes of Warner Pier society were out in force.

The first class is the tourists—people who visit Warner Pier for a day or a week and who rent rooms in the local motels or bed-and-breakfast inns. They were dressed in shorts or jeans with T-shirts—lots of them touting either colleges ("M Go Blue") or vacation spots ("Mackinac Island Bridge"). The tourists wander idly, admiring the Victorian ambiance of Dock Street, giggling at the sayings on the bumper stickers in the window of the novelty shop, licking ice-cream cones and nibbling at fudge, pointing at the antiques ("Gramma had one just like that, and *you* threw it away!"), and discussing the prices at the Warner Winery's shop. They buy postcards or sunscreen or T-shirts, and sometimes antiques or artwork or expensive kitchen gadgets.

The second class is the "summer people," the ones

who own second homes in Warner Pier or along the shore of Lake Michigan and who stay in those cottages or condos for much of the summer. Summer people tend to wear khakis and polo shirts, or other forms of "resort wear." They walk along more briskly, headed for the furniture store, the hardware store, or the insurance office. Lots of the summer people are from families who have been coming to Warner Pier for generations. Lots of them are wealthy; some are famous. They're important to the Warner Pier economy, too, since they pay high property taxes for the privilege of living there part-time.

Joe and I represented the "locals," people who live in Warner Pier year-round. There are only twenty-five hundred of us. The other twenty thousand (I'm overestimating, but not by much) thronging the streets were tourists and summer people.

Locals wear every darn thing. Joe had on navy blue work pants and a matching shirt, an outfit suitable for working in the shop where he repairs and restores antique boats. I was wearing khaki shorts and a chocolate brown polo shirt with "TenHuis Chocolade" embroidered above the left boob. A few Warner Pier locals actually wear suits and ties. A very few. Most dress more like the summer people, except for the artsy crowd. That group goes in for flowing draperies and ripped jeans.

The throng on the street kept Joe and me from exchanging more than a few words as we walked along. When we got within a few doors of TenHuis Chocolade, Joe spoke. "Can I come in and talk to you for a minute?"

"Sure," I said. I opened the door and savored the aroma that met me. Warm, sweet, comforting—pure chocolate. Also chocolate laced with cherry, with rum, with coconut, with strawberries, with raspberries, with other delicious flavors. I never get tired of it.

The two teenagers—Tracy and Stacy—working behind the retail sales counter seemed to be handling the half-dozen tourists who were salivating over the display cases, so I just waved to them and led Joe into my office. The office is a small, glass-enclosed room which overlooks both the retail shop and the workroom where the chocolates are made. The skilled women who produce the chocolates were cleaning up for the day—checking the temperatures on the electric kettles of dark, milk, and white chocolate, washing up the stainless steel bowls and spoons, putting racks of half-made bonbons in the storage room, running final trays of chocolate frogs and turtles through the cooling tunnel.

Lifelike frogs, turtles, and fish molded from chocolate were Aunt Nettie's special item for that season. The small ones—about two inches—were plain molded chocolate, but the larger ones—six or eight inches—were more elaborate. Most of the larger ones were of milk chocolate, with fins and other detailing in either dark or white chocolate. The milk chocolate turtles, with their shells decorated with white chocolate, were especially nice, and the frogs—white chocolate decorated with dark chocolate eyes, mouths, and spots—looked as if they might actually hop.

In the office Joe and I both sat down. "Any chance you could get off early tomorrow?" he asked.

"I could talk to Aunt Nettie. She's planning her big pre–tourist season cleanup project—taking the chocolate vats apart—so she may be here late. I guess Stacy could balance out the cash register."

Joe opened his mouth, but before he could say anything the bell on the street door rang, and I caught a flash of bright green from the corner of my eye. Hershel Perkins was walking in.

Joe had his back to the door, so he couldn't see him. I leaned over and spoke quietly. "Hershel just came in to scrounge his daily chocolate. Let's go back to the break room."

Joe and I both avoided looking into the shop again. We walked through the workroom and into the very pleasant break room. It's filled with homey furniture— an antique dining table and some easy chairs—and on the walls are several framed watercolors by local artists.

But right at the moment the break room was crowded. The ladies who had finished up were leaving, and that room is the passage to the back alley. They were walking through, one at a time and in groups, making a great show of not paying any attention to the business manager and her boyfriend.

Joe frowned, then spoke quietly. "I need to talk to you privately. Could you walk down to the park? I'll buy you an ice-cream cone."

"Let me tell Aunt Nettie."

Aunt Nettie was up in the shop, talking to Hershel. It was a little ritual—she was practically the only person in Warner Pier who acted glad to see him.

"Hershel, you mustn't save that too long," she was saying as I came in. "They're for eating, not looking at."

"Aunt Nettie," I said. "I'm going out for a few minutes."

Aunt Nettie turned her back to the counter. "Certainly, Lee. And I'm just getting a eight-inch frog for Hershel. It's the first one we've sold. He wants it as a mascot for his canoe."

I was astonished. Hershel Perkins came in the shop every afternoon and asked for a sample piece of chocolate. I'd never known him to *buy* anything. Particularly not an expensive molded frog. Stacy—Stacy was the plump one; Tracy had stringy hair—turned around and waggled her eyebrows at me. She was obviously astonished, too.

I smiled at Aunt Nettie. "That's great, Mr. Perkins."

Hershel just scowled.

I went back to the break room. "The roof may fall in," I said. "Hershel is actually buying something. He comes in nearly every day to cadge a sample."

"Why does Nettie let him get away with that?" Joe said.

"She says everyone who comes in the shop gets a sample, and Hershel's no different. I think she feels sorry for him."

"I feel sorry for him, too, and I don't want to argue with him again. But I've got to talk to you. Now. Come on."

I was extremely curious. We went out through the alley door and down to the Old Fashioned Ice Cream Parlor, stood in line behind a half-dozen tourists, then took our cones over a block to the Dock Street Park.

The Dock Street Park is the pride of Warner Pier. It's narrow, but it stretches along the Warner River for a mile. The riverside is lined with marinas and public mooring spots for hundreds of small craft. As usual, the river itself was crowded with boats, which can either follow the Warner River upstream or travel down the river and out into Lake Michigan.

None of the park's benches was empty, so we walked along the dock near the public mooring area. Down the way I saw a knot of people gathered around a spiffy wooden motorboat, and I recognized Joe's 1949 Chris-Craft Runabout. Its mahogany deck and sides shone as beautifully as they had the year the boat was built.

I was surprised to see it; Joe usually drives his pickup to town. If he uses a boat, he uses his 1948 Shepherd Sedan. "How come you brought the runabout in?" I said.

"A guy up at Saugatuck wants to see it," Joe said. "I'm going to take it up the lakeshore. Besides, I'm trying to show it off around the marinas. Since the sale fell through."

The boat's price tag was $20,500. Twice Joe and his banker had celebrated because they thought it had sold. Twice the sale had fallen through.

But Joe obviously didn't want to talk about boats. He stopped out of earshot of the gawkers.

"What's this about?" I asked.

Joe stared at his ice-cream cone—one scoop of French silk and one of pecan praline. "I've got a proposition for you," he said.

Then, to my astonishment, he blushed. And he began to stammer. "That was the wrong word. I mean, I've got an invitation. I mean, if you'd like to . . . Maybe we could . . ."

This was really amazing. I'm the one who stammers around, using the wrong word. Joe is the former defense attorney who could convince a jury to turn loose Attila the Hun.

He finally stumbled to a verbal stop and stared at me, apparently at a loss for words.

"What is it, Joe?" I asked.

He took a deep breath. "I did some work on a cabin cruiser for Dave Hadley—you know, at the Warner River Lodge. So—well, he's offered me an evening out at the lodge in exchange. I thought we could take the Shepherd Sedan up there for dinner. Then we could cruise farther up the river. Or out into the lake, if it's calm. I mean, if the mosquitoes aren't too bad. But—you know—we'd need to do it on a weeknight. Because—well, of how crowded the lodge is on weekends. I thought about tomorrow night. If, that is, if you could get the night off."

It wasn't the most gracefully phrased invitation I'd ever had.

Joe's ice-cream cone was dripping down his hand, and he didn't seem to notice. He flushed a slightly deeper shade. "I sound like an idiot," he said. "But I really want you to go."

He looked at me anxiously, and I wanted to laugh.

Or give him a big hug. Joe obviously wanted this to be a big romantic evening, and his awkwardness made it plain that he really wanted me to go.

Didn't he know how complimentary that stumbling and stammering was? Because Joe really *was* cool. If asking me to go to the Warner River Lodge for dinner could throw him into tizzy . . . If he could make the trip into an event, with a ride up the river . . . It meant my answer was important to him.

Which was both gratifying and surprising.

"Lick your ice cream," I said. "When do you want to leave?"

Joe grinned from ear to ear and hauled an arm back as if he was going to yell "Yeehaw!" the way us Texans do. Instead, he exuberantly threw his ice-cream cone about fifty feet out into the river. Then he used his clean hand to squeeze mine. I was sure he wanted to kiss me, but hand-holding is as big a display of affection as I'm likely to get from Joe on a public sidewalk in a public park.

Joe and I had been edging into romance for nearly a year, but it had been a slow journey, and our final destination was still unknown. We both were hauling a lot of emotional baggage, mainly connected with our former spouses, and events such as murder had thrown even more obstacles in our way. For months we hadn't done anything but talk on the phone.

Finally, late in February, Joe had invited me out in public. Since the night we'd made our official appearance at Dock Street Pizza—social center of Warner Pier, Michigan—all our friends and relations had regarded us as a couple. I was twenty-nine and Joe was thirty-three; they assumed we were ready to settle down.

But we weren't a couple yet. And there were a lot of pitfalls in the way of our becoming one.

The first was money, and that was largely my fault. I have a horror of debt which I developed by watching money problems break up my parents' marriage, and my feelings about money only grew more complicated after I married a wealthy man who thought he could buy a solution to any difficulty. Since I knew Joe didn't have a lot of money, I wouldn't let him spend much on me. Seeing him pull out a credit card to pay for dinner ruined my whole evening.

Money bothered Joe, too. By now his buddies from law school were buying big houses and taking European vacations, and he must have had moments when he regretted leaving the practice of law. Because of his legal problems involving his ex-wife—who died deep in financial doo-doo and without changing an old will which made Joe her executor—he could only work part-time on his boat business, so it wasn't growing very fast.

Plus, our living arrangements put a lot of traps in the pathway to romance. Joe lived in one room at the boat shop and cooked with a hot plate and a microwave. His décor included a roll-away bed and a worn recliner. Because of this, he didn't like to invite me over. I shared a house with my aunt. I'd asked Joe over to dinner a few times, but Aunt Nettie insisted on retiring to her bedroom, where she tried to be quiet. Joe and I sat in the living room, uncomfortably aware of her presence.

Then the tourist season hit, and I started working from noon until around ten p.m. We had a lot of problems just scheduling dates.

But the biggest pitfall may have been that we both recognized that we weren't in this for a casual fling. Maybe we were making excuses to keep each other at arm's length. Maybe the truth was that we were both scared.

Our situation was very much up in the air. Sometimes I got really impatient. Dating Joe was like reading a book when I was simply dying to know how it would end. But I couldn't turn to the back page to find out.

It had been a long, cold winter and spring. But now the weather had warmed up enough for a trip up the Warner River in Joe's favorite wooden boat. And a client had offered Joe dinner for two at a snazzy restaurant, so I wouldn't feel compelled to lecture him about wasting money. I thought I could get an evening off. No wonder the two of us stood there looking into each other's eyes and beaming more brightly than Michigan's summer sun.

Then a cloud crossed Joe's face. He yanked my hand. "Come on!" He pulled me along the dock. "Here comes Hershel."

I looked at the boats beside us. One was a bright green canoe with the words "The Toadfrog" on the prow. "Yikes! We're right beside his canoe."

Joe and I walked down the dock at a brisk pace.

"Hershel never wears a life jacket," I said. "Maybe he'll drown himself on the way home."

The remark didn't seem so funny twenty-eight hours later, when Hershel's canoe was found smashed and half submerged in the Warner River.

Chapter 2

We almost ran up the dock to the next sidewalk, then cut back through the park, toward Dock Street. Joe was still holding my hand, but he was frowning. "I don't understand what got into Hershel down at the post office," he said. "I've never had any quarrel with him."

"How have you missed? He's quarreled with everybody else."

"I avoid him. In the past whatever bee he's had in his bonnet hasn't caused our paths to cross. Until now. Because I'm not backing down on the Root Beer Barrel. I'm going to sell that property."

"But why should Hershel care?"

"Who knows why Hershel does anything? Why did he picket the Superette two years ago, wanting them to put a warning label on all products containing refined sugar?"

I had lived in Warner Pier only a year, so this was news to me. "You're kidding! And he snags chocolates from Aunt Nettie every day? What does he think sweetens them?"

"Nobody expects Hershel to make sense. Last year,

as you may recall, he devoted himself to an attack on the use of gasoline-powered engines in boats."

"Hence the canoe?"

"Right. I lay low on that one. He didn't seem to realize I repair gasoline engines, so he concentrated his harassment on Green Marine. Apparently his new craze is historic preservation."

I looked back and watched Hershel paddling across the river toward the willows that hid his ramshackle house. His distinctive canoe—the only kelly green canoe on the river—wobbled, since Hershel wasn't much of a canoeist.

"I hope we've heard the last of Hershel for a while," I said.

Aunt Nettie agreed easily with my plan to take Tuesday evening off.

"You and Joe need more time together," she said. "If the girls have any questions, I'll be here. I'm planning to start cleaning the vats about four o'clock."

"You're sure I don't need to help?"

"No! I want you to keep us solvent, not mess around with the chocolate. Go out with Joe."

So at eleven o'clock that night, I was standing in my closet doorway and trying to figure out what to wear the next evening when I went out to dinner at the Warner River Lodge, with the prospect of a boat ride afterward.

My fragrance would be simple to select—mosquito repellent would fill the bill. Formal dress would not be required; Warner Pier is a resort, after all. I decided to wear cream-colored slacks, a cotton sweater in a soft green, and a shirt printed with green fronds on a cream background. Joe had once told me that sweater made my eyes look green; he seemed to consider it a compliment. Plus, it was an outfit I could wear tennis shoes with, and rubber-soled shoes would be best in a boat.

I went to work at eight-thirty the next morning. Aunt Nettie showed at one p.m. Beginning at four, she tore up the entire workshop—the chocolate making area—as she superintended the cleaning of the chocolate vats.

TenHuis Chocolade depends on having a ready supply of melted chocolate for the bonbons, truffles, and molded chocolate we produce. So we keep a vat of each kind of chocolate ready all the time. These are TenHuis-sized vats, of course. They're nothing like the enormous vats the Hershey plant would need. But the vats still range from four to five feet tall and are a couple of feet in diameter. The smallest one—for white chocolate—holds one hundred seventy-five pounds of chocolate. The dark chocolate vat holds two hundred pounds of chocolate, and the milk chocolate vat two hundred fifty pounds.

The vats are made of stainless steel and are something like giant thermos bottles—vats within vats. The inside vat holds the chocolate, and the outer vat holds hot water. An electrical element keeps the water at an even temperature, and the water keeps the chocolate at an even temperature. The top to the inner vat opens so that solid chocolate can be dropped in, but when Aunt Nettie or one of her helpers needs to take chocolate out, they use a tap and run the melted chocolate into a pitcher or mixing bowl, just like getting water from the sink. Inside the vats are paddles which churn gently twenty-four hours a day.

Those vats are boogers to clean. All the chocolate has to be drained—which means you have pans and kettles of chocolate sitting around the shop getting solid. The paddles and other internal parts have to be scraped down, then washed by hand in hot, soapy water. The hot-water vessels have to be drained and the water replaced.

Fortunately, the job doesn't have to be done very often. Aunt Nettie insists that it be done early in the summer, before the heavy tourist season starts and before she and her crew begin producing the first Halloween items.

It was a good thing Aunt Nettie didn't need my help. I spent the day in a dreamy state, making even more verbal faux pas than usual. I handed some tourist a dark chocolate bonbon with a white dot in the center of the top and told him that I'd give him the raspberry, leaving out the word "cream" ("Raspberry Cream—Red raspberry puree in a white chocolate cream interior, coated in dark chocolate"). Then I asked Tracy to check the supply of mocha perimeters, instead of mocha pyramids ("Milky coffee interior in a dark chocolate pyramid"). The worst one was when I reached into the display case for a Midori coconut truffle, and at that moment Stacy asked me if Joe and I were going out that evening. I nodded and said, "We're rolling in coconut." This was a reference to the truffle I was picking up ("Very creamy all-white chocolate truffle, flavored with melon and rolled in coconut"), but don't ask me why the chocolate's description worked its way into my reply.

Luckily, the answer cracked both Stacy and me up— something about picturing Joe and me rolling in bushels and bushels of Angel Flake—and we laughed the rest of the afternoon. Every time we quit one of us would start again. The customers must have thought we were nuts. Coconuts.

We were still snickering when a plump brunette walked in the door. I didn't know her, but I immediately classified her as a member of the Warner Pier art colony. Something about her flowing draperies and folksy beads.

Stacy spoke to her immediately. "Hi. How's your summer going?"

"Racing by, Stacy," the brunette answered. "Racing by. But today I'm hunting my brother. I don't suppose he's been around?"

"No—unless he came in this morning." Stacy turned to me. "Did you see him?"

"I'm sorry," I said. "I don't know whom we're talking about."

"Oh!" Stacy looked astonished. "This is Mrs. Waterloo. She's my English teacher."

Thank goodness I'd said "whom." And I'd certainly misjudged her profession. But Waterloo? Was this Mrs. *Frank* Waterloo? If so, she was a sister to the cranky Hershel Perkins. I regarded her warily. Was Hershel's crankiness a family trait?

But the plump brunette was smiling in a most uncranky way. She did have thin lips and a wide mouth like Hershel's, but on her the family feature became generous and humorous. She did not resemble a frog at all.

"You're Lee McKinney, aren't you? We haven't met. I'm Patsy Waterloo." She extended a hand that was covered with rings—the handcrafted kind. "Hershel Perkins is my brother. Nettie is always terribly patient with him. I know he's not much of a customer."

"Mr. Perkins bought a big frog yesterday," Stacy said. "First one we've sold."

"But he hasn't been in today," I said.

Patsy Waterloo made a face that was half-friendly and half-dismayed—I guess you'd call it a grimace. Then she moved down to the end of the counter and cocked her head, beckoning me to join her. When I did, she spoke again, dropping her voice almost to a whisper. "You're the girl Mercy Woodyard's son has been pursuing, aren't you? Pardon me for being such a nosy bitch."

I laughed. "Nobody else in Warner Pier apologizes for being interested in their navels—I mean, their neighbors! Yes, I'm seeing Joe."

"Have you talked to him today?"

"No. Why?"

Mrs. Waterloo's grimace became more concerned than friendly. "Well, we haven't seen Hershel since last night."

"Oh, does he live with you?"

"No, he lives next door. But he usually eats dinner with us. Anyway, after that scene in the post office . . ."

Her voice seemed to fade away. She turned around, draperies swirling, and nervously walked up and down, back and forth in front of the counter. Then she leaned over, very close to me, and spoke more softly than ever. "Hershel was still talking wildly last night. About Joe. I thought he'd gone home to bed. But this morning . . . his bed hadn't been slept in."

"If you're worried, I could call Joe."

"I tried to call him, but he's not answering the phone at the boat shop."

"I'll try his cell phone."

I went into the office, and Patsy Waterloo followed me. I guess her concern was catching. I had only Joe's landline on my speed dial—he normally uses the cell phone just to call long distance—so I had to punch the numbers in. The moments until the phone began to ring seemed terribly long, and the rings seemed to be five minutes apart.

But there were only two rings before the phone was picked up. "Vintage Boats," Joe said.

"Are you OK?"

"Everything's OK if you haven't changed your mind about tonight."

"Oh, no! But . . . Patsy Waterloo is here. She wanted to talk to you." I abruptly handed Mrs. Waterloo the telephone. As I did I heard Joe's voice again. "The teacher?"

Patsy Waterloo was looking more cheerful. "Yes, sir, the teacher and sister of the village idiot. Hershel Perkins."

Now Joe's voice was just a murmur. Patsy listened

a few seconds, then she spoke. "Oh, I know that's too strong a term for Hershel. His actual diagnosis is minimal brain damage caused by a birth injury. But Hershel hasn't been around bothering you, has he?"

She listened some more. "Well, I'm glad to hear it. We try to control Hershel, but he can be a problem. And you know how he roams around."

Again she told the story of her brother's wild talk during dinner the night before and of her discovery early that afternoon that he had apparently never gone to bed the night before. "We don't know where he is," she said.

Joe's voice rumbled, and Patsy Waterloo frowned. "I know, I know, Hershel is regarded as entirely harmless. And he's never done anything beyond annoying people before. That's why Frank and I were so surprised yesterday when—according to Frank—he actually hit you."

More listening. Then she shook her head. "But that's what worried us. It's so unlike Hershel to do more than simply talk wildly."

She handed the phone back to me, then sank into one of my extra chairs.

"I'm back," I said to Joe.

"Are you scared to go up the river tonight?" he asked.

"It seems as if the river would be pretty safe," I said. "You haven't seen Hershel?"

"No. The phone hasn't even rung today. I'll meet you at the dock around five thirty."

Joe hung up, and I turned back to Patsy. "So Joe hasn't seen Hershel. I wonder where he could be."

Patsy had regained her cheerful air. She stood up, draperies flying. "I know I'm being silly. But Hershel . . . well, you know he's odd. Everybody in Warner Pier knows he's odd. That's one reason Frank and I came back here after Mother died. We figured that here, where people knew Hershel was odd but harmless, it would be easier to control the situation. But I can't help worrying. Especially when he roams around."

"Why does that worry you?"

"We discover him prowling around, asking nosy questions. He annoys people. You can't blame them. So I worry."

She moved toward the door, then turned back, smiling sadly. "Hershel will always be my little brother."

I tried to say a few reassuring words as I walked to the door with Patsy Waterloo. She seemed like a nice person, and her problem with Hershel made me glad I'm an only child.

There was a lull in retail customers, so I began to try to get my balance sheet caught up. In between addition and subtraction I thought about Joe, and I forgot Hershel completely.

At exactly five o'clock Aunt Nettie came up front from the workroom, carrying a big spoon covered with dark chocolate. She stood in the door of my office and looked at me accusingly. "You're off duty," she said. "Go away."

I laughed. "I guess I'm outta here," I said.

I closed out my computer, then went back to the alley and got the green and cream outfit from my van. I changed clothes and freshened my makeup in the restroom. I even took my hair out of its businesslike queue and brushed it hard, trying to make it look smooth and sexy. After all, there's no point in being half Dutch if you don't flaunt your naturally blond hair now and then.

Having made myself as beautiful as possible, I waved at Aunt Nettie, went out the back door, and walked over to the dock to meet Joe.

I was, I admit, a bit excited. Joe had planned a big evening for us. I wanted it to go off well.

When I got to the docks, Joe's personal antique boat—the Shepherd Sedan—was easy to find. Antique boats are always the center of a group of people pointing and asking questions.

A "sedan," as Joe has explained it to me, is a roofed boat. His Shepherd was manufactured in 1948 by a Canadian company. It's a twenty-two-footer, and its hull is mahogany, burnished to a lustrous brown through weeks of sanding and varnishing, more sanding and varnishing, and even more sanding and varnishing—a total of ten coats of varnish, each sanded by hand before the next one went on. Elbow grease and patience are the keys to restoring old boats, Joe says.

The Shepherd's roof mimics the shape of automobile roofs in the late 1940s. The front window is Plexiglas. The side windows are safety glass and they roll up and down, just like the windows in automobiles of the day did. The roof itself is of molded plywood, covered with canvas. The dashboard and steering gear are remarkably like an automobile of the 1940s as well.

In fact, Joe had told me the steering wheel was actually manufactured for a car.

Joe has spent hundreds of hours working on the sedan, and the result is a gorgeous boat with a mahogany hull and an off-white roof. It doesn't really have a cabin, since the back is open, but the roof makes it a great craft for either cool or sunny weather. The Shepherd Sedan may not fly over the water like a Cigarette boat, true, but it's pure class.

When I made my way through the knot of people looking the boat over, however, I saw a problem. Trey Corbett was sitting in the stern.

He was leaning forward, talking earnestly. His stance made him look nerdier and more middle-aged than ever.

When I saw him, Hershel Perkins immediately flashed through my mind—I guess because Trey had been a witness to the altercation at the post office the day before. So the sight of Trey didn't make me happy.

I stopped beside the sedan, which was parallel to the dock and a few feet below it. Joe looked up and grinned, but Trey didn't seem to realize I was there.

"You know the river so well," Trey said.

"Not as well as a lot of other people," Joe said.

"We need your help, Joe."

Joe just shook his head. He extended his hand toward me, then led me down the dock for two steps, until I was opposite the step pad, that rubberized gadget that gives you enough traction to step into the boat gracefully, instead of falling in awkwardly.

Trey finally noticed that I was coming aboard. He leaped to his feet. "Oh! Hi, Lee."

"Hi, Trey."

Joe ignored Trey while I stepped into the stern of the boat. He guided me under the roof and up to one of the two front seats.

Trey stood up, looking worried. "I hope we find Hershel soon," he said. "I really need to be working on the fireplace at the Miller house this evening. I'm giving it a faux marble look, and there's nobody around to do it the way I want. I worked on it all yesterday evening."

"Maybe he'll turn up all right," I said.

"Listen, Trey," Joe said. "Considering the altercation Hershel and I had yesterday, I really don't think I ought to get involved in any search for him. Besides, I promised Lee a nice dinner and a boat ride tonight."

"But, Joe . . ."

Joe shook his head. "No, Trey. I'm not joining any search party. But Lee and I are going up the river, since we've got reservations for dinner at the lodge. If I see a bright green canoe floating by, I'll make sure Hershel's not under it."

Chapter 3

Trey left, but he didn't look happy about it.

Joe cast off the lines that held the sedan to the dock, assuring me I didn't need to help, then sat down behind the wheel of the sedan.

"What makes Trey think Hershel's capsized?" I said.

"He and his canoe are both missing."

"Patsy Waterloo didn't mention the canoe. She just said Hershel was gone."

Joe reached over and squeezed my hand. "Forget Hershel. I am really glad to see you. If you'd backed out of this little trip—well, I think I might have done something desperate."

"Cut your suspenders and gone straight up, as my Texas grandma would have said? But why would I back out?"

"It just seems as if everything else that's happened for the past twenty-four hours has failed to turn out the way I wanted it to."

Joe started the motor and the boat began burbling. The motors of old boats are cooled by pumping water around the engine, and the design gives them a distinctive sound—a bubbling, murmuring, lush sound that lots of people find the most attractive thing about them.

We pulled away from the dock and moved gently out into the river. All of the dock area, of course, is a no-wake zone, so Joe kept the speed slow and steady. This meant the engine was not terribly noisy, and we could talk, if we yelled. I leaned over Joe's shoulder. "What went wrong?"

"Oh, last night was a fiasco. A wild goose chase."

"You were going to show somebody the runabout?"

"Yeah. Some guy called, said he had seen the runabout at the South Haven show. Said he wanted to look at it, give his wife a ride. Said he was really determined to buy it. So I chased clear up to Saugatuck in high waves and went to the house he described—and nobody was there."

"Nobody was there?"

"Not only that, the house he directed me to—one of those right on the water, with its own dock—it's empty. The neighbors said nobody's been there for two summers. And the owner's name is not the same as the man who claimed he wanted to buy the boat. It was some kind of hoax."

"That's awful! Why would anybody do a thing like that?"

"I have no idea. I was afraid I'd find the shop burned down when I got home, but everything was okay. It sure did ruin my evening. I had to beat the waves back down to Warner Pier."

Handling a small boat in fairly high waves isn't easy. You have to head into the waves, which points your prow away from the shore and means you're basically traveling sideways. Then when you go over the top of the wave, you suddenly swing the wheel toward the shore—or is it away from the shore? I don't understand the process at all, and even Joe considers it a struggle.

"I didn't get back until way after dark," Joe said.

I slid my hand onto his shoulder. "Tonight we'll just be on the river. No waves."

Joe grinned. "All we'll have to look out for is weeds, mud, and other boats."

The Warner River is about a quarter of a mile wide at Warner Pier—which is one reason it was a good place to build a pier, I guess, when Captain Hoseah Warner decided to do that a hundred and fifty years ago. Still in the no-wake zone, we traveled slowly up the river, past the house Captain Warner built in 1850—now a bed-and-breakfast inn; past the pseudo-Victorian condos which sell for a half-million each; past Hershel's funny little house, which always reminds me of the witch's cottage Hansel and Gretel found. For the first time I noticed the bigger, restored Craftsman-style house behind Hershel's. Now I realized that must be Patsy and Frank Waterloo's home.

Joe guided the boat out into the main channel and stepped up our pace. Joe's a very safe boater, but he likes to rev it up and run his boat all over the lake or the river at top speed; it's a guy thing. We sped past the entrance to Joe's boat shop, on our left, and the turrets of Gray Gables, one of Warner Pier's historic summer homes, came into view on the right. It wasn't long before the broad glass windows of the Warner River Lodge appeared around a bend. Joe cut his speed way back, and we floated gently alongside the lodge's dock. The dock attendant caught the mooring line, and we tied up. Joe cut the engine and stepped out—he makes it look easy—then held out a hand so that I could use the step pad to get out gracefully.

"We're early," he said. "We can have a drink on the terrace." He grinned. "Behind one of the umbrellas."

Two hours later we'd had drinks on the terrace and a marvelous dinner in the dining room. We came back down the stairs to the dock hand in hand. Joe helped me into the sedan, then tipped the dock attendant. The sun was still up. Once we'd cast off, Joe even gave me a quick kiss. I wanted it to last much longer, but Joe started the motor.

I turned sideways in the passenger's seat and slid my hand around the nape of Joe's neck. He patted my knee as we moved away from the dock, the motor burbling softly. The boat headed upstream. We were alone.

So it was quite a surprise when a sound like the final trump thundered over the river.

"Joe! Joe Woodyard!"

Joe whirled so fast he must have nearly given himself whiplash, and I jumped higher than I knew I could sitting down.

Downstream we saw a large white boat approaching. Its prow was crowded with spotlights, and the roof of its little cabin was loaded down with radar gear and antennas.

Joe cut the motor to trolling speed. "It's the city patrol boat," he said.

I squinted at the boat, looking into the sun. "Chief Jones is aboard."

As a community that straddles a river and abuts a lake, Warner Pier has to be prepared for law enforcement and emergencies on the water. In the tourist season, there's a full-time water policeman who enforces safety regulations on the river, and the city owns a nifty patrol boat which he uses. It's also used to rescue boaters if there's an accident and to drag the river if there's a drowning. But the chief rarely goes out in the boat, and ordinary boaters who are obeying the rules and minding their own business—as Joe and I had been—wouldn't normally be hailed by the city patrol boat.

"What do they want?" I said.

Joe didn't ask until the two boats were alongside. "What's up, Chief?" he said. "I hope you're not going to haul me into the big search for Hershel's canoe."

Chief Hogan Jones looked grim. "Nope, Joe. We're

not looking for Hershel's canoe any longer. His body, maybe."

"His body!" I yelled, and Joe made a surprised exclamation.

"Yep," the chief said. "We found his canoe caught in some purple sedge near the entrance to your place, Joe."

Some police chiefs really know how to spoil a romantic mood.

Chief Jones sure spoiled Joe's. His face got nearly as dark as his hair, and his jaw clenched and unclenched more often than it had while he was eating his prime rib and steamed baby asparagus in the dining room of the Warner River Lodge.

But there was no help for it. We had to turn downstream and follow Chief Jones back to Joe's boat shop.

Vintage Boats is in an isolated spot at the end of Dock Street, barely inside the city limits of Warner Pier. The area is pretty close to rural. It's heavily wooded, like most of western Michigan, a quality which gives a Plains person like me a spooky feeling. Joe had few neighbors, and those few couldn't see his shop for the trees.

The shop itself is very ordinary, just a big metal building not too different from my dad's automotive garage in north Texas. The building is heated and well insulated, of course, since Joe works in it all year round. It even has some air conditioning, a rarity for such a shop in Michigan, because Joe sometimes has to close part of it up in the summer to keep dust out of his varnish. It has one main room, forty by eighty, with a couple of fifteen- by twenty-foot rooms at one end. One of those was the office and the other was the space Joe had made into a rudimentary apartment. The only sign of luxury in it was a fancy sound system he said was left from his bachelor days—before he made the marriage he always refers to as "stupid."

The shop is not a boat house. It's a hundred feet

from the water, but Joe does have a dock on the river. A gravel drive enters the property from Dock Street, circles the building, and leads down to an area where he can launch a boat.

There are a lot of trees and bushes, but no landscaping. No grass to mow, no flower beds to weed. And there are about a dozen antique boats lined up on one side—each covered with canvas or plastic tarps. These represent a big part of Joe's money woes—he agreed to buy them before his ex-wife died and landed him in the middle of her legal and financial problems. If he can ever get back to his business full-time, the collection of antique boats has the potential to make him a lot of money. But until then, they're just so much junk he has to make a bank payment on every month.

Joe's dock is equipped with a boat lift, a sort of big cradle that can lift a boat out of the water. The lift is covered with a canvas roof. This allows Joe to keep one boat ready to go in the water all the time. Right at that moment, the boat lift held the 1949 Chris-Craft Deluxe Runabout, the boat Joe was trying to sell. He usually kept the sedan tied up on the other side of the dock. Any other boats he wanted to take for a ride had to be hauled to the river on trailers and put in the water just the way my daddy puts his bass boat in Lake Amon G. Carter, down in North Texas.

Most small boat shops, I've found out, are not on the water. In Warner Pier, they're certainly not. The waterfront property—either on the river or on the lake—is too expensive to waste on workshops; it's all occupied by apartments, marinas, B&Bs, restaurants, resorts, and high-dollar homes. Joe had been able to hang on to his property, known locally as the "old Olson shop," because it was on the outskirts of town and had not yet attracted the eye of a developer. But the time was coming when he might find it wiser to do without a private dock than to keep paying taxes on a piece of property worth more than enough to pay off the mortgage. I knew he'd sell if he got a good offer.

As the sedan neared the dock we saw that the area had become the center of the search for Hershel. A couple of skin divers were in the water, and several boats were standing by. One of Chief Jones's patrolmen, Jerry Cherry, was on Joe's dock rigging up lights, though it was still at least an hour before sundown.

Joe idled the sedan's motor and glided up to his dock. Jerry came over and took our bow line and wove it around the mooring cleat on the dock. Joe stepped out onto the dock, leaving me behind. He was polite to Jerry, but I knew he was still mad.

"I'll open the place up, Jerry," Joe said. "You can use my electricity." He walked toward the shop.

Jerry held out a hand to me and gave me a yank as I stepped onto the dock. "Have they found anything?" I asked.

"Just the canoe."

"Where was it?"

Jerry pointed toward the channel. "Out there. Caught in some sedge. About where Maggie Mae—I mean, Meg—is."

"Maggie Mae?"

"Trey Corbett's wife. We called her Maggie Mae in high school. She's in the boat."

"Which boat are you talking about?"

"Trey's boat. The *Nutmeg*."

Jerry wandered off, and I stared toward the boat he'd indicated. It was not big, as Warner Pier boats go—maybe a twelve-footer. I'd become conscious of the length and types of boats since I began to date Joe. But Joe wouldn't have been interested in this boat because it was fiberglass. He had a sign on the door of his office that proclaims the wooden boat fan's manifesto: "If God wanted us to have fiberglass boats, He would have made fiberglass trees." No, Joe wouldn't have given Trey Corbett's boat a second glance.

However, any guy might well have given a second glance to the woman in the boat. She wasn't dressed sexy. In fact, maybe "well bred" would have been the best description. Her regal air turned the khaki shorts and navy sweatshirt she wore into basic black and pearls. She had a little-girl prettiness. Her hair was artfully streaked with blond and had been cut short by a master stylist.

The lights flashed for a moment, and I realized that Joe and Jerry Cherry had the Warner Pier Police Department's floodlights ready to be used. I looked back toward the boat shop and saw Joe and Jerry walking toward something bright green. Something that was balanced on a couple of saw horses. It had to be Hershel's canoe.

I started to join them, but I took one more look at the *Nutmeg* and saw that the boat was coming toward me. Meg Corbett called out, "Lee!"

She evidently knew me, even if I didn't remember meeting her. I stood still until she guided the boat alongside, then took the line she tossed me and wrapped it around one of the dock's piers. I expected her to get out, but instead she stood still and extended her hand toward me, apparently expecting me to shake it. Or maybe kiss it. I picked shaking.

"Hi, Lee. We haven't really met, but I'm Meg Corbett. I think you know my husband."

"Sure. Trey and I are both on the chamber's Economic Deployment—I mean, Development!—the Economic Development Committee. What can I do for you?"

Meg's face wore a strange expression. I decided she was pretending to look sympathetic. The mouth was the right shape, but her tiny little pupils gave the whole thing away.

"Actually," she said, "I was going to offer you a ride home."

"A ride home?"

"Or to your car. Or wherever you want to go."

"I wasn't planning to go anywhere."

"Well, this isn't going to be very pleasant."

I looked around the scene. I didn't stare at Joe particularly, but I thought about him. I didn't want to leave until I found out what was going on.

"I'm too curious to leave," I said. "Joe will see that I get home."

"If he's able to." Meg's voice had developed a smirk.

"What do you mean?"

"The police may want to question him."

"Why?"

"Hershel's canoe was found right outside his boat shop. They're going to wonder why he didn't report it."

"The answer to that is obvious. He must not have seen it."

Meg Corbett shook her head slowly. "It would have been impossible to miss."

I stared at her for a moment. "If he had seen Hershel's canoe, why wouldn't Joe tell the police?"

"He might have reasons. Joe has always had a secretive side." Meg's ladylike veneer was slipping rapidly. "I know that he and Hershel had a fistfight in the post office yesterday. I know that Hershel seems to have left home last night determined to see Joe again. I know that Hershel's canoe was found near Joe's dock, right where Joe takes his boats in and out."

Meg gestured vigorously, apparently forgetting she was standing up in a small boat, and the *Nutmeg* bounced from side to side. She sat down suddenly and not too gracefully in one of the upholstered seats. Then she tried to look smug. "If I were a policeman, I'd have a lot of questions for Joe Woodyard."

I resisted the temptation to reach down, grab the side of her boat, and turn it over. "But you're not a policeman," I said. "And Chief Jones knows Joe. Besides, Hershel wasn't exactly an expert canoeist. We all expected him to have an accident someday."

Meg's voice was ominous. "If this was an accident."

I decided I'd talked to Mrs. Corbett long enough. I didn't say good-bye. I walked away. If Meg wanted either to get out of her boat or to shove it back into the river, she'd have to do it without me.

I walked over to Joe and Jerry. Now I could see the gold lettering on the prow of the smashed aluminum canoe. The *Toadfrog*.

But Jerry was pointing at something quite a way back from the prow. "It's this big dent in the middle of the canoe, Joe," he said. "I hate to say this, but it looks for all the world like somebody in a power boat ran old Hershel down."

CHOCOLATE CHAT

GODS GAVE MANKIND CHOCOLATE

- The Olmec probably domesticated cocoa. Known to most twenty-first century folks as the creators of those enormous stone heads, the Olmec developed a civilization which existed from about 1500 BC to 500 BC, centered on the coast of the Gulf of Mexico, in the area where today's Mexican states of Veracruz and Tabasco are. Olmec territory was extremely fertile, and they grew a wide variety of crops—maize, beans, squash, chili peppers. Chocolate was very likely among them.

- Both the Mayas and the Aztecs had myths that the foods which mankind needed to survive were brought from beneath the surface of the earth by the gods. Cacao is listed in ancient manuscripts as being one of the foods the gods provided.

- Ancient Americans served most if not all chocolate in the form of drinks. Numerous painted pots and carvings show people pouring chocolate from a pot held at shoulder height into one on the floor, a process which produced froth.

- The Aztec and Maya had many recipes for preparing chocolate. Almost none were sweet. Chili peppers were one ingredient of such drinks. Others might have been maize, vanilla, and numerous other spices and herbs. Some of the drinks were served hot, but cold or room-temperature was more likely. Chocolate was for the elite and was rarely drunk by common folk.

Chapter 4

No wonder everyone was assuming Hershel had drowned. If something hit the canoe that hard, anybody in it would have been thrown into the water with terrific force.

At least I now understood where Meg Corbett was coming from. She obviously had seen the canoe. And she'd apparently already made her mind up about what happened to it.

Then she'd jumped to a completely mistaken conclusion.

I slid my arm inside Joe's.

"Well, Jerry, the damage shows you Joe didn't have anything to do with this," I said.

Jerry looked at me, frowning slightly, and I went on.

"If Joe ran into a camel—I mean, a canoe! If Joe ran into a canoe, he'd be in one of his boats, right?"

"Guess so."

"So that proves he didn't do it," I said.

"I don't follow you there, Lee."

"Joe's too good at herding a boat to run into one by accident," I said. "And there's nothing Hershel—or anyone else—could do that would make Joe risk putting a scratch on one of those boats on purpose. Those boats are his babies."

Jerry chuckled.

"Aw, com'on, Lee," Joe said. "You're nearly as important to me as the '49 Runabout."

Joe, Jerry, and I stood there staring at the beat-up canoe. I didn't feel as cheerful as I'd tried to act.

I knew Joe could never hurt Hershel on purpose. Even the day before, when Hershel had actually attacked him in front of witnesses, Joe had merely grabbed Hershel and pinned him against the wall of mailboxes.

As for Joe injuring Hershel in self-defense, Hershel was too ineffectual to be any real threat to Joe. Joe was bigger, smarter, stronger, and more athletic than Hershel. Unless Hershel had brought along a weapon. And if Joe had hit Hershel or otherwise done something to him because Hershel had a gun or a knife, Joe would have immediately called the police.

I completely shrugged off the possibility that Joe had run down Hershel's canoe by accident. Joe really was too good at handling a boat to do that; certainly to do that without noticing that he'd hit something. Again, if he had had an accident Joe would have called the police immediately.

Thinking Joe might be involved was silly, and I resolved not to be a party to any such speculation.

Having made up my mind, I noticed noises from behind me. Joe, Jerry, and I all turned around.

Meg hadn't shoved her boat off, she'd gotten out of it and had walked up the bank in our direction. The patrol boat was just touching its nose to the dock, and as I watched Chief Jones jumped out. He nearly overshot and went into the drink on the other side. I was so annoyed that I didn't even feel sympathetic. And Trey Corbett had appeared from someplace, maybe the patrol boat. Chief Jones recovered his balance, and he, Trey, and the ultra-gracious Meg walked toward us.

"Better not touch the canoe, Joe," the chief said.

"I'm keeping my hands to myself," Joe said. "Who found it?"

"Trey did," Meg said. She sounded proud. "He searched both sides of the river from Warner Marina to Gray Gables. You know, his family's summer place."

Actually, I hadn't known Gray Gables was Trey's family's summer place. Gray Gables was a real showplace. I knew a rich and prominent Corbett family owned it, but I hadn't associated Trey with that particular branch. Trey never acted rich or prominent; he acted like a struggling architect specializing in restoring Victorian houses. Very interesting. I filed the relationship away for future contemplation and attended to the conversation.

Joe turned to Trey. "Exactly where was the canoe?"

"Up against the sedge," Trey said. Purple sedge has a pretty flower later in the summer, but don't admire it in front of a Michigan native. It's an invasive plant—not originally part of the Michigan ecosystem—and it's pushing a lot of the native plants out of the state's wetlands and streams. It grows thickly along the Warner River. I listened as Trey carefully described the spot where he'd found the canoe.

"I couldn't have missed seeing it," Joe said. "It definitely wasn't there when I left."

Joe and Trey would have dropped the subject, I think, but Meg joined the argument. She had regained her ladylike demeanor, and she spoke firmly but with dignity. "If Trey says that's where he found it, Joe, that's where it was."

"Maybe so, Maggie Mae, but it wasn't there before five o'clock."

Meg looked down her nose at Joe, which was a hard trick since she was five five and he was six one.

Joe looked at her coldly. I guess they would have stood there glaring all evening, but Chief Jones spoke. "It could have drifted down there after Joe left," he said. "That's not the question."

Joe shifted his stare to the chief. "I guess you haven't found anybody who saw how the canoe was damaged."

"Nobody's come forward. Of course, we want to find Hershel—find out exactly what happened to him—before we jump to any conclusions."

"And I gather nobody's found any sign of him yet."

The chief sighed. "We found a life jacket. It was floating farther down the bank. A hundred yards upstream from Green Marine."

Trey spoke then. "Hershel never wore his life jacket."

"Right," Chief Jones said. "The river patrolman had spoken to him about it, but it didn't do any good."

"We need to keep looking for Hershel," Trey said.

"Oh, we'll keep at it," the chief said. "And we're calling in the state crime lab to look at his canoe."

The whole bunch of us swung to look at the *Toadfrog.*

"It does appear as if a much bigger boat hit it," Joe said.

"That's one question for the crime lab," the chief said. "This is the other one."

He pointed toward the canoe.

At the spot where the canoe was smashed in most severely, traces of red were visible.

Behind me, Meg gasped. "Blood?" she said.

"Don't be silly," I said. "If the canoe was in the water any length of time, blood would have washed off. That red has to be paint."

Like a chorus line, we all swung the other direction. And there, suspended in the boat lift beside Joe's dock, was the Chris-Craft Runabout, the boat Joe had been running up and down the river the day before, the boat he had been trying to sell, the one he had taken up the lake to Saugatuck to meet a potential buyer. It hung there, beside the dock, a foot out of the water. We could all see it clearly.

The deck and upper part of the hull were burnished mahogany. But below the waterline the boat had been painted a bright red.

We all stared at the boat for a long moment. Then I spoke angrily.

"I suggest you take a paint sample from the Runabout. That should settle the mattress."

That got everybody's attention. The chief, Meg, Trey, Jerry Cherry, even Joe—all of them quit staring at the boat and turned their attention to me. Every jaw dropped.

"Matter!" I said. "That should settle the matter."

Chief Jones chuckled, and Meg smirked, but Joe was the only one who laughed out loud. Which was unusual. He ordinarily ignores my verbal tumbles.

He put his hand on my shoulder. "I need to take care of something in the shop," he said. "Lee, come and help me. And, Chief, if you want a sample of the paint on the Runabout—help yourself. Try not to chip it too badly."

With what dignity I could recover, I followed Joe into the shop, picking my way among the overturned hulls, the wooden hoist that can lift a boat half the size of a yacht, and assorted tools, ladders, saws, cans of paint, and brooms. "What do you need me to do?" I asked.

"Stand guard."

"Stand guard? Why? What are you going to do?"

"Make a phone call. One I want to be sure isn't overheard."

Joe went into his office and picked up the phone. He put it to his ear and clicked a few buttons, then glared at the instrument.

"The darn thing isn't working," he said. "No wonder I didn't get any calls all day today."

"Patsy Waterloo said she called you several times and didn't get an answer, but I figured you'd been out. Can you use your cell phone?"

"Sure. Just stand by the door and warn me if anybody comes."

I stood in the office door, staring toward the other end of the shop. The door we'd come in was open, and I could glimpse the action outside. I could hear Joe as he made his call.

"Mike," he said. "You know that agenda item you had in mind for the breakfast meeting tomorrow? We'd better forget it for now."

Mike? Was Joe talking to Mike Herrera, the mayor of Warner Pier? Mike, who dated Joe's mom?

I continued to wonder while Joe sketched the situation at the shop, describing where Hershel's canoe had been found and telling about the damage to it.

"No, there's no sign of Hershel," Joe said. "But you can understand the situation out here. I'm suspect number one. We'd better put that possibility on hold for a few days."

He listened again. "Sure, Mike, you're right. Hershel could still turn up. But looking at that boat— well, I'll be surprised if he turns up in one piece. Anyway, the canoe was found near my dock. So if you could hold off until they figure out what happened . . ."

His voice trailed off. He listened again, then laughed harshly. "Thanks for the vote of confidence. I'll be in touch."

He pushed the OFF button on his phone.

"What was that all about?" I asked.

"Oh, a little discussion item Mike had for the city council workshop," Joe said. "Where's the directory? I need to call the phone company."

"First you'd better make sure it's not your own telephone that's sick."

"I guess you're right. I'll borrow a phone from Mom and check it."

"But what's this deal with Mike?"

"Nothing much. What I'm wondering is, did someone call the Waterloos?" Joe walked around me, then out into the shop and toward the door that led to the dock and the search for Hershel. Leaving me with my mouth open and no words coming out.

"Did someone call the Waterloos?" he'd said. I thought we could trust Chief Jones to take care of that. In any case, the Waterloos had nothing to do with why Joe had been talking to the mayor of Warner Pier.

Joe had flatly dodged my question about why he had called Mike Herrera.

I could have popped him. I was so curious that I almost ran after him and demanded to know more. Then I decided against it. After all, Joe and I still had secrets from each other. I told myself that I had no right to demand that he tell me all his business. But I sure wanted to know.

I bit my tongue and went back outdoors, where I found Joe repeating his question about the Waterloos to Chief Jones.

"I got hold of Frank, and he was going to find Patsy and bring her over," the chief said.

The Waterloos showed up five minutes later in a beat-up and rusty old Dodge sedan. Frank was at the wheel, and he skidded to a stop in Joe's gravel parking lot. Patsy— still in her flowing draperies—jumped out and ran toward Chief Jones, tripping over the gravel in her sandals.

"Oh, Hogan! Have you found him?"

"Not yet, Patsy. We'll keep looking until it gets dark."

Patsy hugged herself and shivered all over. "I just can't believe Hershel actually capsized. I worried and worried about him and that canoe. But somehow he always seemed to get home safely. Even when we found out he hadn't come home last night . . . I still felt he'd turn up all right."

Frank had joined her. "Is there any way to expand the search, Hogan? Hire divers? Charter more boats?"

"I don't think there's anything else to do, Frank," Chief Jones said. "It's going to be getting too dark to continue the search pretty soon. But the water patrol volunteers are on top of things."

"You know that Hershel had—has—plenty of money, and this would be a legitimate expense for the trust," Frank said.

"I think this is one problem that can't be helped by throwing money at it," Chief Jones said. He patted Patsy on the shoulder. "Do you have a jacket? It's getting cool."

"I'm not cold," Patsy said. "I just keep shaking."

"It's a nervous reaction," Chief Jones said. He looked around, and he seemed to remember that I was there. "Lee, maybe you could take Patsy inside."

"No! No!" Patsy said. "I want to watch."

"We could sit in your car," I said. I hoped my unwillingness to talk to Patsy didn't show in my voice. "You could watch from there."

Patsy agreed to this, and the two of us went over to the rusty old vehicle. As I climbed into the driver's side I cursed the male belief that women are better than men at dealing with emotional crises. Not that it isn't true. But I hardly knew Patsy Waterloo. I didn't think she'd want to cry on my shoulder.

I did feel sorry for Patsy. That afternoon she'd referred to Hershel as her "baby brother." Her concern had seemed completely sincere. Hershel would have been a terribly annoying relative, but Patsy had made me feel that she loved him despite his problems.

She was still shivering. I looked in the back seat and saw a sweatshirt. With my long arms I was able to reach back and pull it into the front. It was a large, hooded garment with a zipper. I handed it to Patsy. "Here," I said. "Why don't you wrap this around you like a shawl?"

"I'm not really cold."

"Maybe not, but your teeth are rattling. Wrap it around you. It'll make me feel warmer."

Patsy smiled. "I suppose these cool summer evenings seem odd to someone from Texas."

"Oh, Texas has cool evenings. It's just that they come in March, April, October, and November, not June, July, and August."

Her smile faded. "How many boats are involved in the search?"

"At least half a dozen."

"Is Joe helping?"

I didn't know how to answer that one. I didn't want to tell her Joe was suspected of causing the boating mishap that very likely had drowned her brother. "He's helping the chief," I said finally.

"I thought maybe he found the canoe."

"No. Trey Corbett found it."

"Oh? I thought—Hogan told Frank it was near Joe's dock . . ."

"I guess it drifted there. Joe left before five o'clock, and he says he's sure the canoe wasn't there at that time."

"But that would mean Hershel was upstream when the accident happened."

"I guess so."

"But how did he get there?"

"Paddled, I guess."

"But that can't be!"

"Why not?"

"It takes a strong canoeist to paddle upstream when there's this much water in the river." Patsy gave a short laugh. "Hershel is not a strong canoeist. It's a couple of miles from our dock to here. I'm not sure he could have made it this far, much less even farther upstream."

I didn't have an answer to that. We both sat silently, and it gradually occurred to me that Patsy might know why Hershel had attacked Joe—first verbally, then physically—in the post office. Had that happened only a day earlier?

I gulped, thought a few moments, and phrased my question carefully.

"Joe says he had never had any cross words with Hershel before yesterday. Do you know why Hershel was angular?"

Patsy turned to me, looking blank.

"Angry!" I said. "Do you know why Hershel was angry with Joe? Yesterday. In the post office."

"Frank didn't tell me any details, and I tried to keep Hershel from talking about it. Just what did Hershel say?"

"He yelled a bunch of stuff about the old Root Beer Barrel. I never could understand what he was mad about."

"Oh." Patsy sounded as if I'd clarified the whole argument for her. She looked out into the river, watching the boats and divers. "It doesn't matter now."

"Probably not. But did Hershel say anything to you? Did he make any complaint about Joe?"

"Nothing I believed."

"Then there was . . . ?"

Before I could finish my question, Patsy gave a squeal. She yanked at the door handle. "Look! They've found something!"

We both jumped out of the car and went down to the dock. Chief Jones, Jerry Cherry, Frank Waterloo, and Joe were standing there, all looking into the sunset. Out in the river I could see the boats forming a tight circle. The *Nutmeg,* with Trey and Meg Corbett aboard again, was part of the circle.

"What is it?" Patsy said. "Oh, Frank, have they found him?"

Frank put his arm around his wife's shoulder. "I hope not, Patsy. I hope not."

We all watched intently as a diver rolled overboard backward, as lines were tossed into the water, and as boats jockeyed around bumping into each other.

"Can you see it?" Chief Jones said.

I looked at him and realized he had an earphone plugged into his ear and was talking into a small gadget. He was in radio contact with the city boat, maybe with some of the other boats as well.

"Nuts!" he said. "False alarm."

The divers pulled something up. Even from the dock I could tell it was a log. They let it drop back into the water. Patsy Waterloo whirled around and dropped her head into her hands.

Chief Jones went over and patted her back clumsily. "I guess we'd better call it off for tonight, Patsy," he said. "It's getting too dark for the boats to accomplish anything. Maybe we'll have more luck tomorrow."

Patsy looked up, her face all screwed up. "You think he'll be floating by tomorrow!" She made the words an accusation.

The chief didn't answer; he simply walked a few feet down the dock and began to talk into his radio again. The rest of us stood silently as the patrol boat began to haul the divers aboard. Trey and Meg brought their boat over to Joe's dock.

Joe spoke. "Mrs. Waterloo . . . Patsy, I honestly did not see Hershel's canoe in the river when I left. I can't believe it was there."

Patsy wiped her eyes. "It's not your fault, Joe. Hershel was—well, not crazy, but—I could never figure out where he got his ideas. I mean, why would you deliberately knock down the Root Beer Barrel, anyway?"

Chapter 5

I heard Meg Corbett gasp, but I think I simply stared at Patsy for a full minute. I couldn't believe what she'd said. Joe had knocked the Root Beer Barrel down on purpose?

Joe's reaction was much like mine, I guess. He didn't change his expression until Meg gasped, and then he blinked twice. He lowered his head and looked closely into Patsy's face. "Hershel thought I knocked down the Root Beer Barrel?"

"I didn't believe it, Joe!"

"Where did Hershel get that idea?"

Before Patsy could answer, Trey Corbett somehow leaped onto the dock and started talking. "Hershel had a terrific imagination," he said. "I was often amazed at what he'd come up with."

The comment didn't seem extreme to me, but its effect on Patsy Waterloo was—well, inflammatory. She flared up as if Trey had tossed kerosene on her and added a match. She almost shouted a reply. "Yes, Hershel had a wonderful imagination! When he was a little boy—and later on. If it had been encouraged. But it wasn't. He was just criticized and made the butt of the whole town."

Trey stepped back from her attack and nearly fell off the narrow dock. "Patsy, I'm sorry . . ."

"Oh, I don't mean you, Trey! You were one of the few who didn't make fun of Hershel, who didn't mock him." Her eyes flashed around the group. Was it my imagination, or did they linger on Meg?

But it was Chief Jones who drew fire next. He made the mistake of putting his mike away and turning back to our group, and Patsy pounced.

"And you!" She was yelling. "You'd think the chief of police would have some patience with his town's eccentrics!"

"I thought I was patient for a long time," the chief said.

"You threatened Hershel with jail!"

The chief sighed. "Now, Patsy . . ."

"Don't you 'now, Patsy' me. I was the one who had to find Hershel that time. He was hiding up at the old chapel. He only goes there when he's really upset! He was scared to death!"

"I'm sorry, Patsy. But we had to keep him from turning in these crazy reports."

"I could have stopped him. All you had to do was call me!"

"I didn't know that then. You'd just come back. You were in the middle of your renovation. I didn't . . ." Chief Jones stopped talking and scowled at his shoes.

Patsy attacked again. "Didn't what? Didn't want me to know about it?"

"I didn't want to bother you," the chief said.

Frank moved in then. "Patsy . . ." And Patsy turned on him.

"It's all my fault, Frank! I talked you into coming back to Warner Pier. I thought I could handle the situation. Now we've squandered our money . . . ruined our marriage."

Frank grabbed her. I think it was supposed to look

like a bear hug, but it looked more like a stranglehold from where I was standing. He crushed her face into his shoulder. "Shhh! Shhh! We're not going into that now. Just calm down, honey."

Patsy pushed him away. "I'm just so tired of it! I try to meet my family responsibilities, but it's been hard! I thought I could do what Mother asked if we kept Hershel here. I thought the trust could help both of us. But it's turned into a nightmare. Especially for you, Frank."

I stood there helplessly, watching Patsy cry. Then I felt a breath on my neck, and Joe leaned over my shoulder. He whispered. "Get Patsy inside the shop and see if you can calm her down."

I wanted to turn around and glare at him. Another case of the menfolks thinking that the womenfolks can take care of an emotional crisis. But I had to admit he had a point. When Frank had tried to act sympathetic, it only seemed to make Patsy worse. Maybe another woman could help matters. And Meg didn't seem to be ready to offer support. She was hiding behind Trey.

"Patsy," I said, "why don't you come inside with me for a minute. Joe keeps a big box of Kleenex in his office. You and I can sit in there and use it up."

I put my arm around Patsy's shoulder and aimed her at the door to the shop. She didn't move very fast, but I was able to maneuver her inside.

Once I had her sitting in Joe's office chair, with Kleenex in hand, I pulled up a straight chair and sat opposite her. I didn't say anything.

Patsy sniffed. "I'm sorry."

"You're entitled to a good cry."

"It's just been really hard."

"I can see that it has."

"Hershel bothered everybody in town."

I smiled. "He didn't bother TenHuis Chocolade.

Aunt Nettie always acted happy to see him, and he never gave me any problem."

"You're lucky! Meg got the idea—I could have smacked her. But she's that type."

"I just met her tonight, but I admit she didn't make a good impression. What problem did she have with Hershel?"

"She always thinks all the men are after her. She got the idea Hershel was stalking her! It was crazy."

I didn't speak. Stalking is crazy, true, but I didn't think that was what Patsy meant.

"It was Trey he was stalking," Patsy said.

"Trey?"

"Oh, stalking is the wrong word. Hershel got hipped on a new subject. It happened all the time. When Trey was working on our renovation, Hershel would hang around. He lives on the property, after all. Trey was always nice to him."

"Trey seems like a pleasant person."

"He is. I don't know how he got mixed up with that Meg. Her name used to be Maggie Mae, you know. And Trey—well, true, his name is Charles Thomas Corbett the Third, but he was known as Chuck until he took up with her. I think it was her idea to rub everybody's nose in his family connections. But everybody knows he comes from the poor side of the Corbetts. Anyway, Trey explained some things about historic preservation to Hershel—actually treated Hershel like a grown-up. Of course, it backfired. Hershel began going over to their house."

"To Gray Gables?"

"No, to Trey and Meg's house. On Arbor Street. He was only trying to see Trey, but Meg got all excited." Patsy subsided into her Kleenex again.

I thought her outburst was over. If she had told the truth, I had a certain sympathy for Meg. I wouldn't like Hershel hanging around my house. It wasn't as if you could really be a friend to Hershel. He wasn't unintelligent, but he was so unpredictable that he wasn't any fun to talk to.

I heard a tap at the office door, and I turned around to see Joe standing there. "I brought Patsy a cup of coffee," he said.

"Oh, Joe, that was nice of you," Patsy said. "You didn't have to make coffee."

Joe grinned and came into the office. "I didn't. They had a jug of it on the patrol boat. Frank said you didn't take sugar or cream."

Patsy sipped the coffee. "I'll try to straighten up. Then Frank and I will go home."

"Before you go, I'd like to know how Hershel got the idea that I knocked down the Root Beer Barrel."

"I don't know exactly what made him think that. You know how he prowled around town."

"But the Root Beer Barrel came down during the last big snow storm. In March."

Patsy patted her eyes again. "I know. Hershel loved to walk in the snow. Especially along the lakeshore. He told me the Barrel had fallen down before I heard it anywhere else."

Joe thought a moment. "It's at least a mile from Hershel's house to the Root Beer Barrel property," he said. "Just what did he tell you he saw?"

"Hershel never made much sense. It was something about a truck. What difference does it make?"

"It would make a lot of difference to me," Joe said. "It might give me problems selling that property. We'd better tell the chief about it. Can you stand to talk to him?"

Patsy gave a weak smile. "I'll try. I need to apologize to Hogan anyway. He tried to be patient with Hershel."

We went back outside, but Joe, Frank, Patsy, and I stood around waiting while the chief finished up with the water patrolman. By the time he joined us, there was only a little sunset glow left in the western sky and Jerry Cherry's portable lamps were casting a harsh light on the dock. Meg and Trey were gone.

At Joe's insistence, Patsy repeated her story. In fact, Joe cross-examined her. Joe doesn't do his lawyer act too often, but when he does do it, I can see that he must have been good at it. He went at Patsy from six different angles.

But Patsy didn't know anything else, and Frank swore Hershel had never said anything to him about the old Root Beer Barrel.

"Why does it matter?" Patsy said. "I didn't believe it. Apparently Hershel didn't spread it around town. Why do you even care, Joe?"

Joe and the chief looked at each other. "It's the Historic District Regulations," Joe said.

"I've never heard of the city having to enforce a case," the chief said.

"Yeah, it's usually just obeyed," Joe said. "I certainly would never buck the city regs."

"Historic District Regulations?" Frank said. "I know we had to follow them when we renovated Patsy's mom's house. Trey did the design, and he advised us. We didn't have any problem."

Joe nodded. "Trey's an expert on the regulations. They aren't all that onerous, but there's a part that deals with 'demolition by neglect.' In other words, if you own a historic structure and you just let it fall down. That's not allowed. I'd have to look at the ordinance to see what the penalty would be. Then there's a section about deliberately demolishing a historic structure—a property owner couldn't get away with that. He'd have to pay fines. He might even have to restore the demolished structure in some way."

I was confused. "But why would the Historic District Regulations even apply to the old Root Beer Barrel? It didn't have any artistic or historic merit, did it? Not like—oh, say, Gray Gables. That's a real mansion."

"Right, Lee," Joe said. "Gray Gables is worth preserving because it's beautiful—at least to people who like High Victorian architecture—and because it was owned by a famous man—Trey's great-grandfather, the ambassador—and because it's a great example of the late nineteenth century summer home. But as I understand the ordinance—and I studied it pretty carefully—ordinary structures are also covered."

"You mean all that stuff Hershel said at the post office . . . ?"

"Yeah. Hershel was right. Vernacular architecture is considered worth preservation. An unusual business structure like the Root Beer Barrel would definitely be included. That's the one of the main reasons that section of Lake Shore Drive hasn't been redeveloped since the road fell in."

Joe turned to Patsy. "Believe me, I did not allow the old Barrel to deteriorate on purpose."

"I didn't think you did, Joe," Patsy said. "You only became the owner last fall, right?"

"I'm not really the owner at all. The owner is Clementine's estate. I'm just the executor. The estate acquired the property as settlement for a debt. But it was of limited value, because the ordinance required that the old Root Beer Barrel be preserved. I admit I gave a loud 'hurrah' when the storm blew the thing down. But I didn't help it along."

We all stood silently, contemplating the fate of the old Root Beer Barrel. Then Chief Jones spoke. "At the time, nobody suggested that the Barrel had any help coming down. I don't know how we could figure out what happened to it now, three or four months after it happened. I'll talk to Trey and some of the other experts. But as Patsy says, it probably doesn't matter at this point."

The circling boats had left by then. Patsy and Frank drove off in their SUV, and Jerry Cherry and the chief began to load up some equipment. The trees all around were closing in on me. I moved a little closer to Joe.

He spoke to me quietly. "I guess I need to get you home."

"Do you?"

"Our romantic evening is completely shot."

"I guess so. At least we had a good dinner." I led Joe inside the shop, out of sight of the chief and Jerry Cherry. "May I have a goodnight hug?"

Joe obliged. He expanded the hug to include a kiss. And another kiss.

"I guess we don't have to take a boat ride," I said.

Another pause. "We could go by the shop," I suggested. "The break room ought to be deserted. I could make coffee."

"Well, it would make an awful nice interlude before I go to jail," Joe said. "Could I have a double fudge bonbon?"

" 'Layers of milk and dark chocolate fudge with dark chocolate coating.' You could have two."

"Yum, yum. I'll have to lock up."

"I could help you."

Joe and I went back down the dock, and he fastened the sedan in its proper place, locking its mooring chain. Chief Jones and Jerry called out good-byes, promising to be back early in the morning.

Joe followed the chief to Jerry's car. "If I'm not around, and you need to get into the shop, there's a key in a magnetic case behind the drain pipe at the corner of the building." He pointed to the corner he meant.

We waved, and the Warner Pier police car drove away. Joe and I watched as their lights disappeared behind the trees that surrounded the shop. Then we got in Joe's truck, alone at last. I moved over to the center of the truck, and Joe put his arms around me. We sat there several minutes, fully occupied with each other. The windows of the truck were rolled up. It was really dark.

Then I gasped. "Oh!"

"What's wrong?"

"I left my tote bag in the sedan."

Joe nibbled my ear. "I guess you need it."

"I guess so."

He nibbled again. "I'll get it for you."

"Thanks. I'll be waiting."

Joe fished a large, square flashlight out from under the seat of the pickup, then got out of the truck. He closed the door. I could hear his footsteps crunching over the gravel and could see the beam from his flashlight bouncing over the ground as he walked around the side of the shop. Then the light disappeared, but I could still see it reflected overhead on those scary trees. The sound of Joe's footsteps faded away, and all I could hear was the night insects.

Then a voice hissed out of the darkness. "Miss McKinney! Miss McKinney!"

Someone rapped on the passenger's side window.

Chapter 6

If I didn't wet my pants, it was because I was too busy trying to restart my heart. It had come to a dead stop. My head, however, whirled toward the sound at the speed of light.

I don't know if I whispered or shouted. "Who's there?"

"It's me. Hershel Perkins." The croaking voice was unmistakable.

"Hershel!"

Oddly enough, knowing it was Hershel outside the truck calmed my fears. Hershel was strange, but I wasn't afraid of him. I rolled the window partway down. "Hershel! We thought you were dead! Where have you been?"

"I'm hiding."

I tried to open the truck's door, but Hershel pressed against it, holding it closed. "No! Don't open the door! I don't want any light."

"Why not? You must be hurt. We need to get help for you."

"I'm not hurt as bad as some folks want me to be."

"People think Joe rammed your canoe. We've got to tell the police you're all right."

"No! I can't trust them."

"Sure you can."

"No! I saw all those people on the dock. They're out to get me!"

"The police? Your sister? Surely not."

"Oh, Patsy might be all right. But there's Frank. I don't know about him."

"Joe was there. He doesn't want to hurt you. And Trey's always been nice to you, hasn't he? They'll be relieved to find out you're all right."

"No! They may all be in it together."

"Why, Hershel? Why would anybody—anybody at all—want to hurt you?"

"I don't know why. But they do!"

Suddenly I didn't want to be alone with Hershel. This was not the harmless crank who had come into TenHuis Chocolade for a free treat every day. This was a new Hershel, one who feared other people, who might strike out, thinking he was protecting himself.

"Joe's just on the other side of the shop." My voice almost trembled. "He'll be back in a minute."

"I've got to be gone before he comes. The only person who can help me is your aunt."

"Aunt Nettie? How can she help?"

"She's the only one I can trust! Don't tell anybody else. I'll meet her at the old chapel at midnight."

"The old chapel? What old chapel?"

"She'll know where I mean. Midnight!"

Footsteps skittered over the gravel, and Hershel was gone.

Suddenly I could make a noise again. "Joe!" I threw the truck's door open and stood up with my head outside. "Joe! Come quick!"

Immediately I saw the reflection from Joe's flashlight bouncing around in the trees. I heard the *crunch, crunch, crunch* as he ran through the gravel. He yelled, "What's wrong?"

I couldn't make myself get down from the truck.

For a minute I stood there, sticking my head out of the cab like a giraffe. Then I sat back down and slammed the door. Joe would be there in a second. He had his cell phone. He'd call the police. Jerry, Chief Jones—they'd be back lickity split. They'd search the woods for Hershel.

And they wouldn't find him.

It would be impossible to find Hershel in the dark in the woods around Joe's shop. Hershel could hide in those woods. He could climb a tree or lie down behind a bush. He could listen to everything the searchers did, see a lot of what they did.

And Hershel would know I hadn't obeyed his instructions not to tell anyone but Aunt Nettie. He wouldn't keep his end of the bargain and go to the old chapel—wherever that was. But meeting him there might be the simplest way to find him.

Just as Joe reached the hood of the truck I reached a decision. I couldn't tell Joe what Hershel had said. Not there, not at the boat shop, with Hershel still out in the woods. Maybe close by, listening. No, I had to get away from there, find Aunt Nettie and ask her how to handle the situation.

Joe yanked his door open. "What's wrong?"

"I'm sorry," I said. "I guess my imagination got the best of me."

"Huh?"

I spoke loudly and distinctly. "I thought I heard something. I got scared. But I guess it was just an animal."

Joe stood there, staring at me. I'm not usually the clingy type—even when I'm threatened by trees. I could tell he was mystified. But I couldn't worry about that.

"Joe, could we get out of here?"

"Sure." Joe handed me my tote bag and slid behind the steering wheel. He started the truck's motor.

"I need to get the van and head home," I said. I

slid over next to the right-hand door and fastened my seat belt.

Joe turned his head toward me. In the dim light from the dash I could see that he looked more mystified than ever. And maybe angry. But I couldn't help that.

"You sure changed your mood in a hurry," he said.

Yikes! I'd forgotten that I'd offered Joe coffee and chocolate at TenHuis Chocolade. Now I was having to back out. "I'm sorry. But I've got to see Aunt Nettie."

"Your aunt?"

"It's important."

"What's wrong, Lee?"

"Nothing."

"Did I do something? Say something?"

"No! No, I've just got to pick up my van and get home to see Aunt Nettie. Let's go!"

Joe stared another moment. Then he backed the truck around and drove off, down the narrow road that led to the settled part of Warner Pier.

Once we were away from the shop, I opened my mouth, ready to tell Joe about Hershel. Then I pictured his reaction. He'd certainly never let Aunt Nettie and me meet Hershel at the old chapel without him. And if Joe was there, Hershel might not come.

And where was this old chapel? Was it the place Patsy had mentioned—the one Hershel went to when he was really frightened? It must be.

I didn't know what to do. I waffled all the way to the shop.

My silent debate was the only conversation that went on. Joe didn't say a word. He is not usually sulky, but he had a right to be mad—certainly puzzled—by my sudden about-face, building him up for a late-night tête-à-tête, then changing my mind. But I was too frantic about how to deal with Hershel to worry about him.

When we drove down Peach Street, past TenHuis

Chocolade, I saw lights inside. "Oh. Aunt Nettie's still here!"

"Why would she be there so late?"

"I don't know. I hope nothing went wrong with the big kettle cleanup. Just pull up in front."

The minute the truck stopped moving I opened the door and got out. "Thanks for the ride."

"Lee!"

"I can't talk, Joe."

I started across the sidewalk, and Joe jumped out of the truck and followed me. "Lee! What came over you? Did I do something wrong?"

"No! I've just got to see Aunt Nettie."

"Why? I want to know what's going on."

"Nothing's going on!" Inside the shop, back in the workroom, I could see Aunt Nettie. She was standing beside the dark chocolate vat. On the work table behind her I could see several big stainless steel bowls.

"Lee . . ."

"Joe, I've got to go."

I yanked away and turned toward the front door of the shop, but before I could get there, a terrific bang rang out.

"Lee!" Joe jumped about six feet, grabbed me by the arms and shoved me up against the brick wall beside the door. "Get down!"

"Joe! Let me go!"

"That was a shot!"

"It was not! Aunt Nettie is breaking chocolate!"

Joe backed off slightly. "Breaking chocolate?"

"Breaking chocolate. We got stuck with some chocolate that comes in ten-pound bars. They can't go into the chocolate vats until they're broken up."

"I never heard that noise around the shop before."

"We usually get chocolate in little bits—almost granules. But our supplier substituted bars. Let me go, please."

Joe moved away, scowling.

"I'm sorry, Joe," I said. "I know I'm not behaving rationally. But I thought of something while you were getting my bag, and it's vital that I talk to Aunt Nettie about it."

This time Joe didn't argue. I went into the shop and closed and locked the door behind me. I didn't look back at him.

The aroma of warm chocolate enfolded me, and Aunt Nettie looked up. "Lee? What are you doing here?"

"Something came up. I had to see you right away."

"My goodness! I hope you and Joe didn't have a fight."

"Sort of. But that's not the important thing."

"Back when I was dating your uncle, a fight would have been the most important thing in my life." She was standing in the middle of the workroom, beside a big sheet of white paper which had been laid on the floor. As I came into the work room she picked up a white package about a foot long. She lifted it over her head, then hurled it onto the paper. *Bam!* She leaned over and picked up the package. Its contents were now obviously in pieces.

"Oh, Aunt Nettie, listen to what's happened." I poured out the story of the missing Hershel, the damaged canoe, the probability that Joe was a suspect, and, finally, Hershel's appearance at the truck's window in the dark.

Aunt Nettie stared at me, idly turning the crumpled package back and forth. Now her eyes were as round as her tummy.

I looked at my watch. "And it's nearly eleven now. Hershel emphasized that he wanted to meet you at midnight. Where is this chapel anyway? How do we get there?"

Aunt Nettie's face took on a look of complete dismay. "I can't go," she said.

I squinched my eyes closed. She must be afraid. I

could hardly blame her. But I had to find Hershel and get him to turn himself in to the chief—or to somebody. It was the fastest way to prove that Joe had nothing to do with running down Hershel's canoe. And it was the fastest way I could think of to get Hershel to a hospital and to treat any injuries he might have.

Somebody had to be at the chapel at midnight. And if I had to go alone, I'd do it.

"Okay," I said. "Just tell me where this chapel is."

"I suppose he means the old Riverside Chapel. It's just about a mile from Joe's shop, and there's a hiking trail along the river. I'm sure Hershel could find it, even in the dark."

"Okay. Can you draw me a map? I'll go alone. I know it's a scary situation."

"I'm not *afraid* to go!"

"You probably should be. Hershel is really talking crazy."

"Nobody could be afraid of Hershel. It's this chocolate. I simply have to get these vats going, or we'll lose a day of work."

I took a deep breath. "How long does it take to get from here to the old chapel?"

"Maybe fifteen minutes in a car."

"Is there a road?"

"Yes. When I talked about the trail, I was thinking of Hershel. He must be on foot."

I checked my watch again. "So we have forty-five minutes before we'd have to leave."

"Yes."

"Okay," I said. "Tell me what to do, and we'll get as much done on the chocolate vats as we can. But I'm dragging you out of here at twenty to midnight. Meeting Hershel at that chapel is the quickest way to prove Joe did not run his canoe down, and I'm finding that guy and bringing him back."

Aunt Nettie smiled. "Wash your hands, and I'll tell you what to do."

I took off my green sweater and put a big bib apron on over my cream slacks and green and cream shirt. I tucked my hair into a food service hairnet. I washed my hands in approved food service fashion—even turning the water off with the paper towel so that my clean hands didn't touch the fixture. Aunt Nettie told me to get a knife and start digging chocolate out of the big bowls.

"Just put a few pieces of the chocolate back in the vats at a time," she said. "Remember, chocolate melts easily—the melting point is only ninety-two degrees. But we have to be careful not to put too many pieces in at once. That could jam up the paddles."

I eyed the pans of chocolate warily. None of them was very full, but the chocolate in them looked solid. The chocolate obviously had been out of the vat for several hours.

Aunt Nettie moved over beside the dark chocolate vat, climbed on to a kitchen step stool, and ripped open the package of chocolate she'd just shattered on the floor. She began putting the chunks into the vat.

"First, you can break up three or four more bars of dark chocolate," she said.

I whammed the ten-pound bars into the floor, then set the packages—now filled with chunks of chocolate— aside. Next I worked on the white chocolate—the smallest kettle—chipping the now-solid chocolate from the bowl on the worktable into pieces and feeding them into the vat. While I was waiting for the white chocolate to melt, I worked on the pan of milk chocolate. Aunt Nettie was concentrating on the dark chocolate.

Through all this I was frantically checking my watch, and at twenty-five to twelve I gave Aunt Nettie a five-minute warning. By twenty minutes to twelve we had all three chocolate vats going. There were a lot of dirty pots and pans in the sink, but I got Aunt Nettie into her sweater and out the back door.

She shook her head as she climbed into my van. "I don't understand why Hershel wants to see me," she said.

"He's highly suspicious of everybody—including his sister and her husband. You've always been nice to him."

Aunt Nettie sniffed. "I never thought a chocolate now and then would mean a trip to the old Riverside Chapel in the middle of the night."

"Just tell me how to get there."

"Head up Dock Street to Fifteenth."

"It's before Joe's shop, then?"

"It's farther, but you don't pass Joe's shop to get there. Turn off Dock Street on Fifteenth, then turn right at a corner with a big white house. I think the street is Elm."

"It would be a tree."

Aunt Nettie laughed. "I don't understand why you dislike trees so much, Lee."

"Some of my best friends are trees. I don't dislike them individually. It's only trees in mobs."

"You'll see whole crowds of trees before we get to the Riverside Chapel. It's way back in the woods. Lots of people think the woods up that way are beautiful."

"I'm sure they are beautiful. I can admire the patterns sunlight makes on the forest floor. Stuff like that. It's just that when you're surrounded by trees you can't see the horizon. They get you all mixed up about which way is north. And you never know what's hiding behind them."

"On the other hand," Aunt Nettie said, "if you need to hide, it's handy having a tree you could jump behind."

"Well, you know the joke about the West Texas boy who went to visit the big woods of Minnesota," I said.

"I guess not."

"When he got back, someone asked if there wasn't

some mighty pretty country up there. And the Texan answered, 'I don't know. There were so many trees I didn't see a thing.' "

Aunt Nettie and I were joking about our differing feelings about trees because we were nervous. Heading out into the deep woods to meet the town crank at a ruined chapel at midnight is not my favorite activity. In fact, stated like that, it was absolutely stupid. I thought wistfully of having Joe along—a big, strong guy who knew the terrain and who was smart and who could wrestle and who had a cell phone. Right at that moment I was wishing I'd invited him to the party.

But if Joe had been there, I reminded myself, Hershel probably wouldn't show up.

"See the big white house?" Aunt Nettie said. "Turn right."

We had already been driving down a heavily wooded blacktop road, and our right turn—once we were past the big white house—took us into the real woods. The blacktop became gravel, the road narrowed, and the trees closed in. They met overhead and choked the ditches, crowding in on the road. I had to struggle to keep my teeth from chattering Aunt Nettie's voice was soothing. "It's not more than a half mile," she said. "I haven't been up here in years."

"What is this place? This Riverside Chapel?"

"Originally, it was a boys' camp, I think. There are some cabins and some sort of pavilion that must have been the dining room. When the camp closed down, a group of the summer people started a nondenominational chapel there."

"Like the Lake Shore Chapel?"

"I think that's what it turned into. This location was so remote that the congregation found a more central site and built a real building."

"So the old chapel was just abandoned?"

"As far as I know. Oh, people used it for picnics

or family reunions. But there's no plumbing—or maybe just a well."

"And it's posted," I said. I stopped the van with the headlights on a sign. "Private Property," it read. "No Trespassing."

"I don't think we can let that stop us," Aunt Nettie said.

"It certainly wouldn't have stopped Hershel," I said. "According to Patsy Waterloo, he prowls everywhere—all around Warner Pier."

"I think she's right. I know I've seen him over on our road and on the beach, just trudging along. I wouldn't go so far as calling him a window peeper—but . . ."

"But he spies on people, I gather." I took a deep breath and edged the van forward. "At least the old chapel doesn't seem to have a gate."

I had spoken too soon. Around the next bend in the road a barred gate appeared. "I'll open it," Aunt Nettie said. Before I could say more than, "Aunt Nettie . . .", she was out of the van and over to the gate. She shoved at it. It wiggled, but it didn't open. She came back.

"The gate's padlocked. We'll have to walk from here. I hope you have a flashlight."

We'd come this far; neither of us was going to balk at going the last few feet. I reached into the bin under Aunt Nettie's seat and produced a heavy flashlight—the kind my dad says every vehicle should be equipped with.

"I'll leave the van's lights on," I said. "At least we'll be able to find it on our way back."

Aunt Nettie and I climbed over the gate. The road was not graveled but was merely a sandy lane—the type with grass down the middle. The trees, of course, met overhead and were crowding into the road.

"It can't be far," I said.

"It's not. In fact—Lee, shine the flashlight up ahead."

I was terrifically relieved to see a structure less than a hundred feet away.

"We can make it," I said.

I dropped the light back onto the ground immediately in front of us, and the two of us walked up to the building. As Aunt Nettie had said, it was a rustic pavilion suitable for use for picnics or outdoor worship. The roof, which probably had holes in it, was held up by posts—four on each end, and eight down each side. There were no walls, and the floor—I could see bits of cement slab—was covered with matted leaves and other forest debris.

The place was deserted. Nobody called out to us, and I didn't see Hershel standing there waiting. Aunt Nettie stepped under the roofed area, and I used the flashlight to check my watch. "It's five till twelve," I said. "I vote that we don't wait long."

"Lee!" Aunt Nettie's voice was tight. "When you lifted the flashlight—there's something over in that corner. Shine the light over there."

She gestured, and I turned the flashlight where she directed. I saw nothing.

"Farther back," Aunt Nettie said. "It was outside the pavilion, I guess."

She clutched my arm as I inched the light farther and farther away, directing the flashlight's beam to the edge of the pavilion, then beyond. Now I saw something, too. It was a lump, huddled on the ground. I turned the light full on it.

We were looking at a bright green shirt.

Chapter 7

Aunt Nettie and I clutched each other.

"That's Hershel's shirt," I said.

"He's hurt," Aunt Nettie said. "We'd better see if we can help him." She took a step toward the heap.

"Wait!" I grabbed her arm. "Let's look around first."

"But, Lee . . ."

"Hershel can wait another minute," I said. I guess I'd already decided Hershel hadn't been hurt in some kind of accident. I felt sure he'd been attacked, and I wanted to make sure the person who had attacked him wasn't still there waiting for us to lean over Hershel and become easy targets.

I pivoted slowly, shining the flashlight's beam all around the pavilion. I saw nothing. Nothing but trees.

Aunt Nettie shook off my hand and went to Hershel. I followed her.

Hershel was on his back, with his face turned slightly away from us. He looked peaceful, lying there in a clump of ferns. His eyes were open, but the bright light from my flashlight brought no reaction from his pupils. A pool of red had spread beneath his head.

Aunt Nettie knelt and touched his wrist. "He's still

warm," she said. "It's been a long time since I took first aid, but I don't think he has a pulse. I don't think we can do anything to help him."

She spoke very calmly, but I saw that her hand was trembling.

"Let's go," I said.

"I don't think we should leave Hershel here alone."

"I'm certainly not leaving you here with him. And I'm not volunteering to stay myself. We'll have to go back to town and call the police."

"It doesn't seem right."

"Oh, yes, it does!"

I pulled her to her feet, and in the process I nearly dropped the flashlight. It swung around crazily.

And, at the other end of the pavilion, the light reflected on a pair of eyes. Someone was standing there looking at us.

I nearly went into cardiac arrest for the second time that night. Then I forced myself to focus the flashlight on the eyes. And I saw Joe Woodyard leaning against one of the pavilion posts, squinting.

"What the heck are you two doing?" he said.

I've had a lot of emotional ups and down in my twenty-nine years, but right then I felt as if I were on a roller coaster. I was so relieved it was Joe that I could have kissed him and so mad at him for scaring us that I could have killed him. My feelings ricocheted around that pavilion.

But when I spoke, I guess I sounded fairly calm. "Do you have your cell phone?"

Joe reached for his pocket. "Yeah. I'm not sure it'll work up here—the reception on this side of town is iffy. Who do you want to call?"

"The police." I turned sideways and motioned toward Hershel.

Joe gave a low whistle and walked toward us.

"He doesn't have a pulse," Aunt Nettie said. "At least, I can't find one."

Joe checked Hershel's pulse, then listened to his chest and put a wisp of grass beneath his nostrils. "I don't think CPR would do any good," he said. Then I remembered that Joe had been a lifeguard for three summers.

He pulled out his cell phone and punched in numbers. And he didn't punch in 9-1-1. He tapped in a whole string of numbers.

"Who are you calling?"

"City Hall. The dispatcher can hear the answering machine this time of night. It's quicker than getting the wrong 9-1-1. Which is easy to do from a cell phone."

That made sense. But other question flitted through my mind. How had Joe known the number of Warner Pier's City Hall? And why did he know all this stuff about the dispatcher's routine? The question evaporated before it could get out of my mouth. It didn't seem all that important at the moment.

Joe waited, then spoke, apparently to the answering machine. "Hey, Lorraine—are you on duty? Pick up, please. It's Joe Woodyard. We've found Hershel Perkins, and he's dead."

The dispatcher came on immediately, and Joe described exactly where we were. "I think we're still inside the Warner Pier city limits," he said. Trust a lawyer to worry about jurisdiction at a time like that. "Okay. We'll wait here." He put his phone back in his pocket.

"She said she'd get the patrol car and the chief right away," Joe said. "Just what were you two doing up here?"

"We came to meet Hershel," I said. "How did you happen upon the scene? And how did you get to the pavilion without our hearing you?"

"Tiptoed. I was following you."

"Why?"

"After the way you acted, I thought you were up

to something. And I sure hope that answer satisfies Hogan Jones. Because he's also going to wonder just what I was doing up here."

Joe chivalrously offered to stay with Hershel while Aunt Nettie and I went back to the van, but we refused to leave. I explained how Hershel had come up to the truck and told me he wanted to see Aunt Nettie. Then the three of us stood there waiting. The atmosphere was cozier with three of us. It was a long five minutes before we heard a siren, and several minutes later before we saw car lights flashing among the trees.

"That'll be Tom Jordan. I'll walk down and meet him," Joe said. I knew Tom Jordan—an older guy who worked for the Warner Pier Police Department part-time during the summer tourist season. But I hadn't known who was on duty that night. I wondered how Joe had happened to know.

In a minute Tom—his gray hair glimmering in the flashlights—came toward the pavilion, with Joe leading the way. Chief Jones was close behind them. The chief wearily asked Aunt Nettie and me how we'd happened on the scene, then told us to go home. "I'll get your statements tomorrow," he said.

I pictured my van, parked on that one-lane road with its nose right up against the gate. "You'll have to let us out," I said. "I guess there are three cars behind us now."

"Just Tom and me," the chief said. "Who else did you think would be there?"

I turned to Joe. "Where did you leave the truck?"

"There's a little turnoff a couple of hundred yards back down the road," he said. "I nosed the truck in there, in case I didn't want you and Nettie to know I was here."

The chief looked at Joe closely. "You didn't come with Lee and Nettie?"

"No. Lee acted so odd—well, I figured she was up to something. So I followed them."

"But you parked back down the road?"

"Right." Joe sighed. "It doesn't look good, does it?"

I didn't get it. "What doesn't look good?"

The chief shrugged, so Joe answered the question. "Since I'm not parked behind you, I can't prove I arrived after you did," he said.

"But what difference does your time of arrival make?" I said. Then I saw the answer. "Oh!"

"Yeah," Joe said. "I could have been here ahead of you—in plenty of time to kill Hershel. First his canoe was apparently run down near my dock, then I'm on the scene when he's killed. If I were the chief, I'd have me down at the station in a flash."

I wanted to argue, but Joe shook his head. "You'd better get Nettie home," he said.

By this time the patrolman was moving the two Warner Pier PD cars, and I couldn't really justify hanging around. So I backed down the narrow lane to the place where Joe had turned in—the patrolman walked along and showed me where it was—then I turned around and headed back to Elm Street.

We had to go to the shop, of course, because Aunt Nettie's car was parked behind it. And going behind the shop meant going inside, so that she could make sure the big electric chocolate kettles were functioning properly. I almost had to lasso her to keep her from washing the pots, pans, and bowls we'd left in the sink.

"No," I said. "You're going home. You came to work a long time ago. The morning crew can wash the dishes."

Aunt Nettie sighed. "I guess I'm getting old."

"You don't seem to be, but I'm aging fast."

We went home. We got in bed. I didn't close an eye, but morning came anyway.

At seven a.m. the phone rang. I could hear Aunt Nettie in the bathroom, so I ran downstairs and caught the call.

"Lee? It's Trey."

"Trey?" I double-checked the time. Why was Trey calling so early? Why was he calling at all? "What's up?"

"Is it true that you and Joe found Hershel's body last night up at the old chapel?"

"I'm afraid so." I didn't mention Aunt Nettie.

"So Hershel didn't drown?"

"Not unless—" I bit back a snotty remark about a wash tub. "No. It looked like a head injury, but I'm no expert. I guess you and the rest of the river patrol volunteers wasted your time looking for him in the water."

"That doesn't matter! We were home by dark. After Meg and I had a bite, I even went over to the Millers' to work on that fireplace. But I guess you and Joe kept looking for him."

"That's not exactly the way it happened, Trey."

"I'm just stunned. If Hershel had a head injury, I wouldn't have expected him to be able to get to the chapel."

"What do you mean?"

"The chapel's way up on the bluff. If he was that badly injured, I'd have expected him to be found down by the river."

I answered without thinking. "He didn't get the head injury in the boat accident!"

"What do you mean?"

I thought about it. Could Hershel have been that badly injured and still talked to me in the dark, down at the boat shop, coherently? Or as near coherently as Hershel ever talked? Could an old wound have begun bleeding or something? Could a twenty-four-hour-old injury have killed Hershel?

Trey spoke again. "What do you mean, he didn't get the head injury in the boat accident?"

"I don't know, Trey. Maybe he did. I guess I'd better shut up until the chief has taken my statue. I mean, my statement!"

"How did you and Joe think to look for Hershel up there at the pavilion?" Trey chuckled. "Or shouldn't I ask?"

"Why shouldn't you ask?"

"Well, that spot used to be known as quite the lovers' lane." Trey gave a nervous giggle. "Before they locked the gate. Anyway, that's what the locals say."

"I'd never even heard of the place before last night. So I guess I'm still just a summer visitor."

"Joe never told you about it? Seems as if he would have known. Maybe even taken somebody up there."

"I'm sure he was a normal teenager."

Trey snickered. "Well, yeah. I guess Joe has given Warner Pier plenty to talk about over the years. He's played the field. Or that's what Meg tells me. She's the local at our house." Trey snickered again. "Of course, *you* have nothing to worry about, Lee."

Something about that second snicker got to me. It changed Trey's jokes into snide remarks. If Trey could be snide, I decided, I could be snide, too.

I snickered back at him. "Have you asked *Meg* about the old chapel?"

"Meg wouldn't go there!"

"But you said she was a Warner Pier local."

The silence grew so long that I finally spoke again. "Did Meg go to school here?"

"High school."

"High school was a long time ago," I said. "For all of us. I guess I'd better get ready for wolf. Work! I mean, get ready for work."

"I'm sorry I bothered you so early." Trey hung up abruptly.

I was completely mystified. Had Trey called just to gossip about Hershel's death? I supposed that was logical enough—every coffee klatch in Warner Pier was going to be buzzing over the killing of the town crank. But somehow I didn't feel that had been the real purpose of Trey's call.

I thought he was dropping a hint about Joe. Trying to tell me Joe was seeing someone else. Or had seen someone else. But when I'd turned that tactic on him and asked him about his wife, he'd begun to sulk.

Hmmmm. Very interesting.

I made a pot of coffee, got out the toaster, and prepared to waylay Aunt Nettie at the breakfast table. Maybe she knew something about Meg's past.

By the time Aunt Nettie came out in her white pants and tunic, I'd had some caffeine and my brain didn't seem to be quite as foggy.

"Who was on the phone?" she said.

"Trey Corbett. But I can't figure out why he called."

"What did he say?"

"I'm not sure I understood what he said. But when I made a joke about Meg, it completely killed the conversation."

"Ah." Aunt Nettie gave the syllable enough nuances to fill a semester of English lit.

"What does 'ah' mean? Is there something I should know about Meg? Some deep dark secret in her past?"

"I'm sure you know all that's necessary."

"Necessary? Why should anything be necessary? I never even heard of Meg Corbett until yesterday."

"Oh?" That syllable had a lot of nuances, too.

"Aunt Nettie! If I'm about to put my foot in it up to the knee, tell me! Is there something I should know about Meg?"

"Well, back when she was in high school—back when she was Maggie Mae Vanderveer—well, she and Joe dated for a while."

I rolled my eyes. "Is that what's bothering Trey?" Then I opened my eyes wide. "She didn't leave town in scandalous circumstances?"

"Oh, no! I know Mercy wasn't very happy about Joe seeing her. Maggie Mae—Meg—well, she didn't have the best family life. But I don't like to criticize Meg. It would have been easy for a girl from her background to slide into a lax way of life. The way her mother did, if we're honest. But Meg was ambitious. She got herself through college."

"Sounds like someone I know. If Meg had had an Aunt Nettie to put her on the right path, she'd be president."

Aunt Nettie laughed. "She's nothing like you, Lee. And her family's nothing like yours. You never went hungry or were so dirty the neighbors called the welfare department."

"That happened to Meg? Hard to believe somebody so high-toned could have come from trash."

"I don't know for sure. So much of this is gossip I hear from the ladies in the shop. I try not to believe everything they say." She checked the kitchen clock. "I'll get coffee and a roll at the shop," she said. "There's a woman spending the summer in a cottage near Gray Gables. She's writing a cookbook of some sort. She has a really funny name, and Lois Corbett—that's Trey's cousin's wife—asked me to talk to her, and she's coming in this morning."

Aunt Nettie went to work then, leaving me with a lot more questions about why Trey had called.

I'd been aware that Joe existed when I was in high school just because he had been the head lifeguard at the Warner Pier Beach during the three summers I worked for Aunt Nettie and Uncle Phil. But we didn't know each other. Besides, by that time Joe wasn't in high school. He was a student at the University of Michigan. I assumed he'd had girlfriends in high school—most popular and good-looking guys did—but

I didn't remember any of my friends telling me who they were. If Meg, or Maggie Mae, had been around during those summers, I hadn't known her.

By the time Joe and I met twelve years later, each of us had been married and divorced. I'd never quizzed Joe about ex-girlfriends. He'd volunteered the reasons why his marriage hadn't worked, and I'd confided my problems with my ex. Neither of us had offered to detail every romantic encounter we'd had in our past lives. Frankly, that would seem like a pretty dumb thing for either of us to do.

Besides, we weren't engaged or anything. We weren't even lovers—though that would probably come as a big surprise to the gossips of Warner Pier. Our abstinence was based more on fear than on moral qualms. We were both conscious of our past mistakes and timid about committing future ones. Maybe we were both also aware that we lived in a small town. If our romance ended in a dramatic bust-up, we were still going to be running into each other at the grocery store. There were a lot of reasons for us to be cautious, and so far we had been.

Knowing that Joe and Meg had once dated each other did give me a clue to that undertone of antagonism between them that I'd noticed the day before. It could help explain why Meg was so eager for me to see Joe as a suspect in Hershel's death and why Joe had glared at her once or twice and carefully ignored her the rest of the time. Or could that antagonism be a screen for another feeling?

Was I jealous of Meg? Should I be? By the time I got to that question I was upstairs in my bedroom, looking in the mirror. I had to admit that right at that moment I wasn't the most beautiful woman in the world. Tossing and turning most of the night will do that to you. And Meg was attractive. She had even looked good after spending an afternoon out in a boat, helping search for a drowning victim.

I went to the closet and pulled out an outfit that I thought was becoming—a brown and peach plaid skirt and a V-necked cotton sweater in the same peach. To heck with the TenHuis Chocolade uniform—that day I was going to feel good about myself. I headed for the shower.

I spent some extra time on my hair and face. I dug some sandals out of the back of the closet, sandals I hoped would make my legs look long and shapely. The plaid skirt and sweater did give my morale a boost. I ate a couple of pieces of toast and contemplated the day

One thing the day was going to include, I realized, was giving Chief Jones a complete statement on my encounter with Hershel. I decided that I'd better call and see if he wanted me to come by at any particular time.

It seemed as if the chief had been waiting for my call.

"Chief? It's Lee McKinney. Do you want me to come in today and make a statement?"

"Yep."

"When?"

The chief gave a deep sigh. "Right away, I guess. In fact, maybe you can identify the murder weapon."

CHOCOLATE CHAT

COLUMBUS DISCOVERS CHOCOLATE

- The first European contact with chocolate was made by Christopher Columbus during his fourth voyage. On August 15, 1502, at a place called Guanaja on an island north of Honduras, Columbus captured two gigantic Mayan trading canoes. The goods in the canoes included cotton clothing, war clubs, copper pots, maize, and some special "almonds" which the Indians apparently valued highly. Columbus apparently never ate or drank any chocolate.

- The Spanish invaded Yucatan in 1517 and Mexico in 1519. At first they found the strange drink of the country repulsive. But as the Spanish began to eat native foods—and as they began to intermarry with their conquered subjects—they added chocolate to their diet. They often sweetened it with sugar, and they also developed the wooden *molinillo,* a tool which looks something like a pinecone on a stick and which is used to beat chocolate and make it frothy. This replaced the Indians' custom of pouring chocolate from vessel to vessel.

- The Spanish occupiers went back and forth to their native country frequently, of course, but the earliest written report of chocolate being taken back with them comes from 1544, when a Mayan delegation accompanied some Dominican friars on a visit to Prince Philip of Spain and presented Philip with cacao beans.

Chapter 8

I approached the Warner Pier City Hall and Police Department with dread, of course. I couldn't imagine what horrible object had been used to kill Hershel. And I couldn't imagine why Hogan Jones thought I might be able to identify it.

When I saw the weapon, I was completely mystified.

"Jerry Cherry and I were out there at daybreak," the chief said. His tall, skinny shape bent over a table in his office, and he pointed a bony finger at an object which lay there. "Jerry found this," he said.

The object was a rock about four inches around and three inches thick. A simple, rounded stone—one of the millions which vacationers stub their toes on along any beach on the shore of Lake Michigan.

"What on earth makes you think that was used to kill Hershel?" I said. "There are at least a zillion rocks like that on the beach at Warner Pier. What made this one stand out?"

"It wasn't on the beach," the chief said. He was looking tired—he'd probably been up all night—and his weariness deepened the lines in his face and made him look more like Abraham Lincoln than ever. "It was just inside the woods, about thirty-five feet from the pavilion, close to this."

He picked up a paper sack and showed me that it held a rag. It looked like an ordinary red commercial rag—the kind my dad uses to wipe up grease in his garage, and the kind Joe uses to get varnish off his hands in his boat shop. The kind an industrial laundry delivers or Home Depot sells.

"The rag was what got our attention," the chief said. "The preliminary report says there are red fabric fibers in the wound in Hershel's head. And the rock we found with it appears to match the size and shape of the wound. Wounds."

I shuddered away from a picture of Hershel being hit repeatedly. "Why did you think I could identify it?"

The chief used the eraser end of a pencil to turn the stone over. "It's got something written on it," he said.

I looked closely. I could see three letters. "J.R.W." And a date.

It took me a second to realize they were Joe's initials—Joseph Robert Woodyard. At the same time I realized there was a small hole in the top of the stone, and a second hole on the side.

I put my lips near one hole and my hand near the second and blew. Air rushed out onto my hand.

"What are you doing?" Chief Jones said.

"It's a 'lucky'!" I said. "Don't you look for lucky stones?"

"I don't even know what they are."

"They're a TenHuis family tradition. When you walk along the beach, you look at the stones, and if you find one with a hole that goes clear through it— it's a lucky. If you can't see through it, you have to prove it's a lucky stone by blowing through the hole or by pouring water through it. Then you write your initials on it and take it home. I don't know if anybody but us does it. But that's a lucky stone."

"It wasn't so lucky for Hershel. Do you have any

explanation for how this particular stone could have gotten up to the old chapel?"

"I didn't take it up there. I'd never even heard of the place until last night." I sounded defensive, even to myself. I'd already thought of a place I had put a lucky stone with those initials, but I didn't want to say where.

The chief waited silently, looking at me steadily. He wasn't buying my cover-up. I decided to abandon it.

"Okay," I said. "Joe and I took the runabout up the lakeshore one of the first nice days in May. We had a picnic. It was too cold to swim or even to wade, so we walked along the beach, and I found three or four lucky stones, and Joe found one. When we got back to the shop that evening, I put my stones in the back of the van, and I laid the one he had found near the shop's downspout."

The chief nodded. "We found a gap where it looked like one of the stones was missing. The weather had made a little pocket for it."

All of a sudden I was very angry. "So you knew where it came from all along, and you wanted to trap me into saying the stone came from Joe's shop."

"I wasn't trying to trap you. I was trying not to put words in your mouth at all."

"You thought I'd lie to protect Joe."

The chief opened his mouth, but I kept talking. "Well, Chief Hogan Jones, let me tell you that I would not lie to protect Joe."

"Lee . . ."

"I wouldn't lie to protect him, because Joe doesn't need projecting. I mean, protecting! Joe would never have harmed Hershel. I completely deject—I mean, reject!—that idea."

"Calm down, Lee."

"I'm not going to calm down. I thought you were a friend of mine, a friend of Aunt Nettie's. I thought you liked Joe, too."

"I do, Lee. I like all of you. But an investigating officer has to look at all possibilities."

"But you *know* Joe. He's a decent human being! He wouldn't hurt anybody. Besides, what conceivable reason would he have had to harm Hershel?"

The chief gave a little snort. "Face it, Lee. Anybody in the vicinity of Warner Pier might have had a reason to get Hershel out of the way."

"Because he was annoying? That would be a pretty extreme reaction."

"Not because he was annoying. Because he was nosy. He wandered all around town, more or less spying on everybody."

"But he hadn't spied on Joe."

"Not until he brought up all this business about the old Root Beer Barrel being pulled down."

"But that wasn't true!"

"What if it was true, Lee? Joe's had an awful time with his ex-wife's estate. Right?"

"I've never asked all the details."

"I don't know all the details either, but I do know Joe took the Root Beer Barrel property as payment on a bad debt—a debt owed to Clementine Ripley's estate. But the property was virtually worthless."

"Lakefront property is not worthless. Not in Warner Pier."

"But the lot couldn't be redeveloped because of the Root Beer Barrel, right? The Historic District Ordinance required that the Barrel be saved. And that made the property hard to sell."

"That rule was silly. The previous owner had allowed the old Barrel to become dilapidated. Joe was planning to go to the board and ask permission to take it down."

"He might not have gotten that permission. And just at that moment the Barrel happened to blow down."

I was silent.

"A simple coincidence," Chief Jones said.

"Of course!"

"Except that Hershel said it wasn't a coincidence."

"Nobody believed Hershel! Besides, all this happened three months ago. Nobody thought anything about it when it happened. Why didn't Hershel come forward then, if he knew anything?"

The chief shook his head. "I don't understand it, Lee. And I'm not hauling Joe down to the station yet. But when Hershel's canoe is sunk and then Hershel himself is found dead—and both these things happen near Joe's boat shop—and Joe doesn't have an alibi for either event, I can't just say, 'Ol' Joe wouldn't do a dastardly deed like that,' and ignore it. I've got to look at one of the primary rules of detection—'Cui bono?' Who benefits?"

That pretty much ended our conversation. I made my statement, then agreed to come back at noon—when the chief's secretary would have it ready to sign. But I left in a huff. I was furious at the chief's suspicions of Joe.

I was also scared spitless. The chief was right. Joe had argued with Hershel. And he really was eager to sell the Root Beer Barrel property. And he did not have an alibi for either time Hershel had been attacked. The first time he'd been out in the lake on a boat. The second time he'd followed Aunt Nettie and me up to the old chapel—except as he himself had pointed out, he could have been there first.

I had to do something. But what? The whole situation was scary. Joe would never have knocked the old Root Beer Barrel down. I wasn't even sure he'd know how.

At least, I was sure I didn't know how. Who would know? Who worked with old structures and could tell me how to demolish one?

The answer, of course, was Trey Corbett. And he'd hung up on me at seven that morning after he'd implied my boyfriend might be seeing someone else and I'd countered with a similar implication about his wife.

Then Aunt Nettie had handed me the news that his wife and my boyfriend had once dated each other. What did that mean? They went out a few times? Went steady? Were queen and king of the prom?

I knew Meg didn't have Joe's letter jacket, because he'd dug it out of his mother's attic and given it to me, more or less as a joke. I'd hate to think Meg had had it earlier—but high school was a long time ago. Maybe I needed to call Trey and apologize. I mean, Trey and I were both doing business in Warner Pier. We needed to get along, right? We even served on a Chamber of Commerce committee together.

When I opened the shop door and saw the two teenagers behind the counter and the dozen hairnet ladies calmly molding chocolates in the workroom, I felt relieved and comforted. Aunt Nettie was bustling about with her usual happy expression, and the wonderful aroma of warm chocolate filled the air. I concluded that my amateurish work at refilling the chocolate vats the night before hadn't done any harm. Business seemed to be progressing as usual. Tracy was getting a Bailey's Irish Cream bonbon ("Classic cream liqueur interior") for a broad-beamed woman wearing red shorts not quite big enough for that broad beam.

It was tempting to forget poor Hershel, lying dead with rock-shaped wounds in the back of his head. And I might have tried to forget him, if I hadn't been so worried about Joe.

I helped myself to a Dutch caramel bonbon ("Creamy, European-style caramel in dark chocolate") and reminded Aunt Nettie that sometime that day she needed to make a formal statement about finding Hershel. Then I went to the telephone. I got out the Warner Pier Chamber of Commerce directory— all ten pages of it—and found Trey's number. I made a few notes about what I needed to ask him, then I called.

The phone was picked up immediately. Trey's voice said, "Hello."

"Hi, Trey," I said. "I wanted to apologize for . . ."

But Trey's voice was still speaking. "You've reached the office of C.T. Corbett Architectural Services," he said. "Please leave a message after the tone."

I had to gulp hard before I could leave a message. I'd been so psyched up about speaking to Trey that it didn't seem possible he wasn't in his office. I managed to stammer out my name and the TenHuis phone number, then hung up. His secretary must be out. If he had a secretary. Trey's operation didn't seem to be very large.

I remained uneasy. Maybe I should talk to Joe. I stared at the telephone, tapping my finger on the key that would speed dial the boat shop. Then I remembered that Joe's phone was out of order, or it had been the day before. Besides, the chief had probably kept him up all night; he was likely to be asleep.

I punched in the numbers for Joe's cell phone. If he was asleep, surely he would have turned that phone off.

He answered immediately. "Vintage Boats."

Suddenly I had nothing to say. I had no real excuse for calling Joe. I just wanted to hear his voice.

"Vintage Boats." Joe repeated his greeting. One more second and he'd decide I was a crank call and hang up.

"Joe," I said. "It's Lee."

"Are you okay? Haven't stumbled over any more bodies?"

"Not this morning." Better keep this light. "Did the chief keep you up all night?"

"Just until a little after 2 a.m. Then he and Jerry were at the shop poking around before seven. I hadn't slept much anyway. Has he already had you in for a statement?"

"Yes."

"Then you know about the stone they found."

"Yes, he made me identify the initials. Some lucky stone."

"This whole deal with the Root Beer Barrel has been unlucky."

I remembered that I'd told the chief I had never asked about the details of Joe's business dealings. That was deliberate. Money problems—too much, not too little—had been a major factor when my first marriage broke up. I guess I'd shied away from discussing money with Joe because I was afraid we'd argue about it.

But at the moment I needed to be nosy. "Exactly how did you get hold of the Root Beer Barrel, anyway?"

"A guy named Foster McGee owed Clementine money. He's a Chicago insurance executive. She got him off on a fraud charge."

Joe paused, and I prompted him. "So?"

"McGee had paid Clementine only half her fee, so he owed her money, and as you know, she owed me money. McGee owns a condo up here, and he'd been suckered into buying the Root Beer Barrel—didn't realize it wouldn't be easy to redevelop the property. The city began giving him some trouble over letting the property become dilapidated. When the interest he owed Clementine's estate got too high, he offered the estate the property as payment."

"Why did you agree to take it?"

"Because McGee is almost bankrupt and is none too honest. I knew it wouldn't be easy to do anything with the property, but if he went belly-up the estate might never get anything at all. I started preparing a petition, getting ready to ask permission to demolish the Barrel. Then a miracle happened—or so I thought.

The thing blew down. I thanked my lucky stars and thought there might actually be light at the end of that particular tunnel. Especially when a real live potential buyer showed up."

"Who is this buyer?"

"A guy from Grand Rapids—somebody Frank Waterloo works with. He owns a development company up there, and he wants to expand in our direction."

"What does he want to build down here?"

"I don't know. And I don't care. He'll have to comply with the Historic District Regulations, and I don't think the city would go for a McDonald's."

I laughed. Warner Pier's economy depends on its Victorian atmosphere, so the city is extremely picky about what new structures look like. Plus, pressure from local merchants keeps the Planning Commission and City Council notoriously wary of fast food chains. "Yeah, McDonald's couldn't get in, even if they put gingerbread up and down the arches."

"True. As I said, the thing's been a headache all along."

"And now this. But Joe, after three months—they'll never be able to prove whether or not the Barrel was deliberately torn down."

"I know. And I don't think they can prove I killed Hershel either. But if they don't figure out who did do it—well, I'm sunk anyway."

"None of your friends will believe this. It's silly!"

"But it ruins my reputation."

"Your reputation? I never knew you to worry about what other people thought of you!"

Joe was silent for a moment before he spoke. "Sometimes other peoples' opinions can be pretty important."

Then he hung up.

Our conversation hadn't been reassuring. I was more confused than ever, especially by Joe's reaction.

Instead of relying on his friends to believe in him, he seemed more concerned about the opinions of people who didn't know him.

"Lee." I looked up to see Aunt Nettie standing in the doorway. "Do you want to go over to the Waterloos' house with me?" she said. "I stopped by the Superette and bought a ham."

Chapter 9

Food equals sympathy. The universal belief of small town America.

"I could get some coffee and tea," I said.

Aunt Nettie beamed. "That's a good idea."

I noticed that she had changed from her white pants and tunic into light blue slacks and a matching cotton sweater. I was glad I'd happened to dress up a little, though my plaid skirt might be a little short. But Aunt Nettie seemed to think three inches above the knee was okay for a condolence call.

It was a beautiful summer day in west Michigan, which stars at producing beautiful summer days. We stopped at the grocery store—where I bought three pounds of gourmet blend coffee and a big jar of instant tea, drove across the Orchard Street bridge, then turned up Inland Avenue. Nice of the Warner Pier city planners to label the street which led away from Lake Michigan so clearly. If we'd turned the other direction, we'd have been on Lake Shore Drive, the street that eventually led to Aunt Nettie's house.

The Waterloos' drive was full of cars, of course, and since Hershel had lived next door, I wasn't surprised to see a Warner Pier PD patrol car and the Michigan

State Police mobile crime lab along the curb. The chief would be searching Hershel's house.

We parked down the street and walked back past several beautiful cottages—two Gothic revivals, one folk Victorian, and a Queen Anne which was heavy on the turrets and shingles. The Waterloo house was Craftsman, the style that led up to Frank Lloyd Wright. All us Warner Pier folks know this stuff; we can tell Greek revival from colonial revival with only a brief glimpse of a roofline.

When we walked up onto the broad porch, Betty VanNoord, a math teacher at Warner Pier High, opened the front door. Behind her were two other women I recognized from the Warner Pier High School honor assembly I'd gotten roped into attending the day Stacy got a scholarship. Patsy's fellow teachers had apparently taken over hostess duty.

"Thanks for coming," Betty said. "I'll put the food in the kitchen. Patsy's out on the deck."

"We don't want to intrude," Aunt Nettie said.

"Patsy will want to see you," Betty said. "You two found Hershel."

I hadn't considered that aspect. I hoped Patsy didn't want a play-by-play description.

Another teacher led us through the house to the deck. I'd seen the deck from the river, of course. It was a beautiful addition of a twenty-first century amenity to an early twentieth century house. It was like an extended porch and overlooked a lawn which led down to the river. There was a small dock, but no boat.

Frank was leaning on the deck's rail, big and bald as ever. Nearby Patsy, dressed in a new set of artistic draperies, was sitting in a wicker chair. Both got up and greeted us with the obligatory air kisses, while we murmured useless phrases. But they seemed glad we'd come.

One of the teachers brought coffee, and Patsy asked

us to describe what had happened the night before. I gave a general report, slurring over Hershel's disdain for "that bunch on the dock," a group that had included both Patsy and Frank.

"I was afraid to bring anybody except Aunt Nettie to meet Hershel," I said. "He was adequate—I mean, adamant! He was really firm. He wanted to see her and nobody else. Then he ran off into the woods, and I didn't see how anybody could find him unless he wanted to be found."

"Hershel prowled around so much. I guess he knew every foot of the riverbank, and the lakeshore, too." Patsy dabbed at her eyes with a tissue. "When you found him . . . did he look . . . was he . . ?"

Aunt Nettie took her hand. "He looked as if he was sleeping, Patsy."

Patsy nodded, and tears ran down her face. They ran down Aunt Nettie's, too. After all, my Uncle Phil—the man she'd been married to for forty years—had been a homicide victim, too. He'd been killed by a drunk driver. I wouldn't have described Hershel as looking "as if he was sleeping." But if Aunt Nettie thought it would help Patsy to be told that he looked that way, it was fine with me.

I realized I was tearing up, too, mainly because I also missed Uncle Phil. But crying with Hershel's sister made me feel like a hypocrite. I sympathized with Patsy, but I had regarded Hershel as a pain. Pitiable, yes, but a pain. Acting as if he had been a personal loss made me feel dishonest. Finding his body had been a shock, true. But what I was really interested in was the evidence that made Joe look guilty when I was convinced he had nothing to do with Hershel's death.

I eyed Frank, still standing at the rail. Joe had said that the Grand Rapids man who wanted to buy the old Root Beer Barrel was someone Frank knew. Maybe Frank could tell me a little more about the circumstances. Under Chief Jones's rule of "Cui bono?" or "Who benefits?" that guy was a suspect. He wouldn't have wanted to buy the property if the old Barrel hadn't fallen down.

I patted my eyes with a tissue, then got up and took my coffee cup over to the rail, standing beside Frank.

I nodded toward the rustic cabin under the trees, closer to the lake than the Waterloos' house. "Is that where Hershel lived?" Yellow tape surrounded the cabin, and I could see a couple of guys bent over outside, apparently searching the ground.

"Yes. I guess we can redo it as a rental. Something."

"You've done a beautiful job on this house. How old is it?"

"Patsy's great-grandparents built it in 1919."

"It's lovely. Did you do the remodeling work yourself?"

"Oh, no. Trey Corbett was entirely in charge of our restoration project—designed the plan, found the subs, got the work done. Patsy made the final choice on the wallpaper, and I wrote the checks."

"Writing the checks is a major contribution, Frank. Projects like that get out of hand financially real fast."

"I will say that Trey paid some attention to the budget we had. I was nervous about the cost of the project, since he comes from a wealthy family and lots of those people have no idea of the value of money. We still had to scramble . . ." His voice trailed off.

I saw a way to introduce Frank's links to construction, and I jumped in. "Your construction experience must have been a big advantage."

"My what?"

"Your experience with construction."

Frank chuckled. "I have no experience with construction. I can't tell a paintbrush from a band saw. What gave you the idea I know anything about building?"

"Something Joe said. I guess I misunderstood his meddling. His meaning!"

"I think so." Frank held out his hands. "See these? Ten thumbs. I can't drive a nail. What would have given Joe the idea that I had something to do with construction?"

"Oh, he said you know the developer who's interested in buying the old Root Beer Barrel property. That you were business associates. I suppose I deduced that you knew him through construction. But you must have known him through some other connection."

"Known who?"

"I don't know his name. The man who's interested in buying the Root Beer Barrel."

"I'm supposed to know this guy?"

"That was the impression I had. When the Barrel blew down, the man heard about it, realized it would make the property easier to redevelop, and came forward with an offer. He told Joe he'd heard about the property through you."

Frank laughed. "That's small town gossip for you."

"It's not true?"

"No. I was in California visiting my mother when that big storm hit. There may have been some discussion about it around here at the time, but I didn't find out that the old Barrel had blown down for weeks. I definitely didn't tell anybody about it."

"Nobody in Grand Rapids?"

Frank shook his head. "I don't know anybody in Grand Rapids who's in construction or development. I don't know anybody there at all. We only moved here five years ago—when Patsy's mother died. All I've been able to find is a crummy job as night manager in a printing plant. I never get to put my nose out the door!"

"I guess I definitely misunderstood."

Frank frowned angrily. "We only came here because of Hershel. We thought handling the trust ourselves would be easier." He laughed harshly. "And now this!"

I heard Patsy's voice. "Frank . . ."

Frank leaned close to me. "Don't tell Patsy I was griping. We had to move to Warner Pier—and it's fine, most of the time. A nice little town. But now and then I have to blow off steam."

I nodded, and the two of us went back to Patsy. But I was confused by what Frank had told me. Joe had been definite about the prospective purchaser for the old Barrel's plot. He'd said it was someone who worked with Frank.

There was probably a simple explanation. Someone Frank knew, but whom he didn't know was in the construction or development business.

Aunt Nettie and I began to make noises about getting back to the office. But when I looked out toward the river I saw Chief Jones loping across the lawn with his disjointed gait. He carried a paper sack in his hand. He brought it up onto the porch and beckoned to Patsy, who went over to him.

Aunt Nettie and I kept edging toward the door, but I was curious. It was the same kind of sack Chief Jones had put the red rag in. I figured it was some sort of evidence.

"No!" Patsy spoke loudly. "I never saw Hershel with such a thing!"

We all swung to look at her. She looked around wildly, and her eyes settled on me. She took two steps in my direction. "Lee will know," she said.

"What is it, Patsy?" I asked.

She reached for the sack, but Chief Jones pulled it out of her reach. "We don't need to involve Lee," he said. "I can ask Joe."

But Patsy was still talking. "It's a horrible color. Where could Hershel have picked up such a thing?"

She came over and looked at me, eyeball to eyeball. "Joe couldn't do that, could he?" she said. "Even if he came over to Hershel's house, he wouldn't have killed him. Why should he kill my baby brother?"

I was still gaping when she turned and ran into the house. I turned to the chief. "Okay," I said. "Let me see it."

"Don't touch," he said. "We'll check it for fingerprints."

I put my hands behind me, leaned over slightly, and looked into the sack. I saw something a bilious, nasty green. I immediately knew what it was.

"Oh," I said, making my voice casual, but loud enough for all the teacher-hostesses to hear. "It's one of those giveaway pens Joe got to hand out at the wooden boat fictional. I mean, festival! I don't think that a pen like that is conclusive evidence that Joe was at Hershel's house. Those pens are probably all over town."

The chief nodded. "We'll find out," he said.

Aunt Nettie and I left. Despite my attempt at being casual, I was more upset than ever. Because those pens were *not* "all over town."

Joe had bought five hundred to hand out at the wooden boat festival up at Muskegon, and he had deliberately picked the most eye-catching color the novelties company offered. The pens were a perfectly ghastly shade of chartreuse. I hated the color so much I'd refused to have one on my desk. As far as I knew, Joe still had three hundred of them in a box in his desk and a half-dozen in a coffee mug beside his computer. They wrote fine and had good erasers, but the color was so horrible he couldn't even give them away.

Aunt Nettie and I said gracious good-byes and left. We arrived back at the shop to face two reports. Hazel, Aunt Nettie's chief assistant, said that Deer Forest Bed and Breakfast needed four dozen crème de menthe bonbons ("The formal after-dinner mint") so they'd have plenty to put on their clients' pillows every night. Nancy Burton, the owner of the B&B, couldn't leave to come and get them because she was waiting for a plumber. And Tracy, who'd been on telephone duty, said that Trey Corbett had called me twice and seemed extremely eager to reach me. He said he'd call back in twenty minutes.

"Well, I can handle both those problems," I said. "First, if Hazel has the crème de menthe bonbons ready, I'll drop them by Nancy Burton's. That shouldn't take more than ten minutes. Then I'll be here when Trey calls."

At last, a couple of things I knew how to cope with.

Chapter 10

I dropped the mints off, then turned back toward downtown Warner Pier. As I turned onto West Street, I saw the pretty little cottage at the corner of MacIntosh Avenue. It might look authentically Victorian, but it hadn't been there when I was a teenager. Aunt Nettie had told me that Trey Corbett had built it to house his architectural and construction business.

Looking back, I should have kept straight on to the office and waited for Trey to call. But the impulsive side of my nature took over, and I turned into the parking lot. The SUV was there; I deduced that Trey was, too. We could talk face-to-face.

As soon as I was inside the office I began to suspect that my deduction was wrong. The outer office was empty, and I could hear Meg's voice coming from the inner office. I peeked around the corner and saw her talking on the phone. Meg frowned and waved. I mouthed, "I'll wait," and popped back into the outer office.

Darn. I didn't want to talk to Meg. I wanted to talk to Trey, and he apparently wasn't there. But I could hardly leave again without telling Meg why I'd come.

I moved across the office, making sure I couldn't hear her conversation.

The office was beautifully decorated, with furniture in classic styles. No gimcracks, no curlicues, no cute Victorian. Just plain, good design. The front wall was all proper Victorian-style windows, but more of them than the Victorians would have wanted. A giant, abstract oil painting dominated the back wall. One side wall, the one farthest from the office door, was taken up by an object I call a map rack. It's actually a dozen racks, each designed to hold two large maps or drawings, back to back. The racks swing out from the wall like a book when you want to look at them, then swing back flat for storage. Rich Godfrey, my ex-husband, was a real estate developer, and he always had a couple in his office, ready to display plats for potential property buyers.

The map on the front of the rack was a detailed plat of Warner Pier. I wandered over and took a look at it. Yes, there was Peach Street, where TenHuis Chocolade was located. There was the corner where my friend Lindy Herrera lived, Ninth and Cider Alley. I took a close look at North Lake Shore Drive, particularly the area around the old Root Beer Barrel neighborhood. The map didn't tell me anything I didn't already know.

I idly swung the rack to look at the map behind it. But there was nothing back to back with the plat, in the position corresponding to page two in a book. And the "page three" rack didn't hold a map. It held an elevation—an architect's drawing. I recognized it as Patsy and Frank Waterloo's house. It was a beautiful picture. Trey had drawn an idyllic home, surrounded by lush plantings and flowers, and he had tinted the whole thing with dreamy pastels. The elevation was a work of art. In the corner was a neatly lettered title, "Home of Frank and Patsy Waterloo, Warner Pier, Michigan."

I turned to the next rack and saw another elevation. This one was Trey's own office building. The drawing was just as lovely as the one of the Waterloo house. "Office Building," the label read. No details. I turned to the next rack. It was a house I had never seen, though I recognized the style—Italianate. The label read, "Home of George and Ellen VanRiin." I didn't know the VanRiins, but they lived in a beautiful house.

I turned the rack again and again, looking at a half-dozen more lovely drawings of quaint Victorian buildings. All of them were on right-hand "pages," as it were, of the rack. I was sorry when I came to the last one, a drawing of a bed-and-breakfast inn I recognized. I assumed it was the final thing in the rack, but I automatically looked behind it. To my surprise I realized there was one more elevation. This one was on the left-hand rack, back to back with the previous drawing.

This elevation was of a much larger structure than the others. I didn't recognize the building, but again the drawing was beautiful and the colors delicate. In fact, it might have been the most charming drawing of all. The building stretched out over the whole width of the paper. It had tall trees behind it. One section was like townhouses, delightful cottages with steeply pitched roofs. The other end was a three-story building with broad verandas. It looked like a period resort, a relic of some Victorian watering place. It made me long for a floor-length skirt, a pompadour, and a parasol.

I looked at the corner of the drawing to see where it was located. But there was no label, no name, no hint as to what or where it was.

I was flipping back though the drawings when Meg Corbett suddenly shoved herself between me and the map rack. She spoke angrily. "What do *you* want?"

I took a step backward, determined to be nice, even

if Meg wasn't. "Meg, Trey's elevations are lovely! He should have a show of them."

"Trey is very talented. But you didn't come to see his elevations. Why did you come?"

"I wanted to talk to Trey a minute. Is he here?"

"No." Meg began turning the sections of the map rack back, one after the other. "Why did you want to see Trey?"

I almost turned and walked out. Meg was certainly not being hospitable. But I reminded myself that I was a Texan, not a damyankee, and Texans are polite. "I guess I was looking for free technical infection—I mean, information! Like collaring a doctor at a party to ask him about your athlete's foot."

"What did you want to know?"

"How to knock down the old Root Beer Barrel."

"What!" Meg gave me a sharp look, then turned more map racks, banging them back against the wall.

"Everybody keeps talking about how Hershel claimed it was knocked down on purpose," I said. "I just began to wonder how hard it would be to do that. I thought Trey would know."

"I'm sure he would." Meg turned the final map rack. "Trey's gone to Holland. I told him you called and he said he'd return your call on his cell phone."

"He did. I missed the call. Then I was out on an errand and saw that his SUV was here, so I pulled in."

"He drove my car."

"I'm sorry I bothered you."

I turned toward the door, but Meg spoke. "Wait, Lee." When I looked at her, she had changed her mouth from huffy to happy, but her pupils were still tiny and hard. "You and I need to talk for a minute," she said.

"Sure." I decided I could match Meg hypocrisy for hypocrisy. I put on my beauty pageant smile and took the chair she waved toward.

Meg sat in an identical chair. She was wearing another summer visitor outfit—jeans with tennies and a pale blue cotton sweater over a white polo shirt. As she had the day before, she looked almost too well bred. Hard to believe she had been a child so neglected the neighbors called the welfare department.

"I'm sorry I snapped," she said. "We're all upset about poor Hershel."

Her comment confirmed my opinion of her as a real witch with a capital "B." Meg hadn't cared a whit about Hershel. I made my smile even toothier. "What can I do for you?"

"Oh, Trey told me he'd called you this morning, and he was afraid you'd misunderstood."

"Oh?"

"He said he made some reference to Joe Woodyard."

"I hadn't been up long when he called. I'm afraid I wasn't making a lot of sense." I made my smile wide enough for Miss America competition, and I decided to spike her guns. "I didn't understand—was he trying to tell me that you and Joe dated each other in high school?"

"Oh? Had Joe told you about that?" Was it my imagination, or did she look rather disappointed?

"I know about it." I didn't learn it from Joe, but I knew. "I hadn't put a lot of importance on it."

Meg's smile grew as big as mine, and her pupils grew even smaller. "That's a *good* attitude, Lee. Of course, *you* know all the little tricks to keeping a man interested."

"Tricks?"

"Those things we learn at our mother's knee. Keep 'em guessing, never let them feel overly confident about you, things like that."

So Meg thought romantic relationships were based on little tricks. I wasn't surprised, but I found her attitude annoying. I kept smiling. "I've even been known to fall back on sincerity," I said. "When you can fake that, you've got it made."

A frown briefly clouded Meg's perfect eyebrows. She didn't seem to know what to make of my comment. "Well, as long as you understand that there's been *nothing* between Joe and me since high school."

"I don't really worry about ancient history."

Meg simpered. "Well, it *is* ancient history. I didn't want you to think anything else."

"I didn't."

"Though it's gratifying to know Joe *mentioned* me."

"Joe's been around the block a couple of times since high school, Meg. You shouldn't feel too bad if he seems to have gotten over your teenage romance."

Her jaw tightened. "He was really mad when we broke up. But by the time I was a senior, I could see that Joe wasn't really my type. I've told him repeatedly, over the years, that I have no interest in him. And, of course, events have proven me right."

"What events?"

"Well, you know. His . . . lack of purpose."

Was she was referring to Joe's decision to quit practicing law and open a boat shop?

Meg spoke again. "You know, there's no substitute for family background."

That comment confused me further—I didn't know anything particularly disreputable about Joe's family. His parents had been divorced, and his mother ran a successful insurance agency. His father—now deceased—had been a carpenter. His family wasn't rich or famous, but it was respectable. Unlike Meg's had been, apparently. I contented myself with raising my eyebrows at Meg.

Meg's laugh tinkled out again. "Anyway, I met Trey—and, well, I fell for him in a major way. He had all the qualities I was looking for—you know."

I began to think I did know. I was getting the picture of what Meg had been looking for in a husband. I did the eyebrow wriggling bit again. "Family background?"

Meg—well, the only word is "preened." "Trey is intelligent and trained to a profession, of course. But the Corbetts give their sons a top-notch education. There's a family trust dedicated to that purpose."

I couldn't resist a dig. "I understand perfectly, Meg. Trey probably went to prep school . . ."

"Capperfield."

"And to a 'good' college   "

"Hyde."

He'd been to such a good college I'd never even heard of it. I had trouble not making my smile a smirk. "   and he has the family fortu . . . I mean, _connections_! The connections to help him become successful." I leaned forward. "Which has always made me curious. What is Trey doing in a little place like Warner Pier?"

"I beg your pardon?"

"I mean, why isn't Trey practicing architecture in New York, in Chicago, even in Grand Rapids?"

Meg's expression hardened. "His interest is Victorian architecture— and here he's able to indulge it."

"That _is_ lucky."

Meg stood up. "Trey says Warner Pier is the perfect place for him to learn Victorian building practices and design from the ground up. He's written papers on the buildings he's restored here."

"Wonderful."

"Trey's going to knock Michigan on its ear," she said. "He has big plans."

I excused myself. We both waved and smiled our hypocritical smiles as I backed out of the parking lot. I didn't understand why Meg had wanted to talk to me. Was she trying to make me jealous, with her comments about how she'd told Joe to shove off "over the years"?

When I got back to the shop, Trey had called again. This time he had left his cell phone number. I called him, and Trey answered.

"It's Lee," I said. "I'm calling to apologize if I was rude this morning."

"I'm the one who needs to apologize. I shouldn't have called so early."

Apparently Trey wasn't going to make any reference to Meg and Joe. I wasn't going to mention them either. "I needed to be up and doing. But now I have one question for you—if you have time."

"I'm driving down from Holland, Lee. I can talk. Just don't ask me a question so startling that I run off the road."

"I don't think it would startle you. How would you knock down the old Root Beer Barrel?"

There was a moment of silence. Then I heard a horn blare. Yikes! Maybe he had run off the road. "Trey? Are you all right?"

"Yes. But that *was* a startling question. I hope you're using the word 'you' as a general term for humanity, not asking how I actually did it."

I laughed. "I guess I meant it as a general term for people who know a lot about how buildings are constructed, Trey."

"But I don't know a lot about commercial properties of the 1940s. I specialize in the Victorian and Edwardian eras. And I try to keep the structures up, not knock them down."

"I know, Trey. But you were the only person I could think of that I knew well enough to ask."

"Sorry. I never looked closely at the old Root Beer Barrel. I don't know how it was constructed. It might be that a good ram with a bulldozer would have brought it down. Or it might have had to be taken apart plank by plank. Why do you want to know?"

Suddenly I didn't want to go into it. "Just nosiness, I guess. Patsy said Hershel claimed it was knocked down deliberately, and I began to wonder how hard it would be to do that."

"Don't worry, Lee. Nobody but an idiot would think that Joe would take it down."

"Thanks, Trey." This time we both said good-bye politely before we hung up.

That hadn't helped. The whole morning had been confusing. I was at a complete loss about how the rock that had killed Hershel had gotten from Joe's workshop to the old chapel. I didn't understand why Joe thought Frank Waterloo had steered a buyer for the Root Beer Barrel property in his direction and Frank denied it. I didn't understand what Meg and I had been talking about, or why Trey wouldn't at least take a guess about pulling the Root Beer Barrel down. There were a lot of unanswered questions, and I wasn't making any progress at answering them.

I fought down a mad desire for a coffee truffle ("All-milk chocolate truffle, flavored with Caribbean coffee"), went to my desk, took out a yellow legal pad, and wrote down two of the questions.

First, why did Joe think Frank had steered a property buyer his way?

Second, what was the relationship between Meg Corbett and Joe?

These were two questions I could simply call Joe and ask. I might not like the answer I got to one of them, but I could ask them. I picked up the phone.

Chapter 11

Joe answered almost immediately. I didn't hit him with Meg's implications right away. Instead I told him that Frank denied telling anybody about the Root Beer Barrel property.

"He says he didn't even know the old Barrel had blown down for a couple of months," I said.

"So what?"

"Well, I've been thinking about the Barrel, Joe. If Hershel was right, and it was deliberately wrecked, the chief has been thinking in terms of its destruction helping you sell it. But it also made it possible for this guy in Grand Rapids to buy it."

Joe was silent.

"In a property sale," I said, "both parties should benefit."

"You're right. Let's go ask him."

"Go ask him?"

"Sure. I need to pick up a boat in Grand Rapids anyway. We can stop by and see this guy."

"The buyer? Who is he?"

"His name is Tom Johnson. Sounds like an alias. But I've seen his letterhead. Johnson-Phinney Development. Can you come with me?"

"Well, I need to get some work done around here . . ."

"We could leave about three, get to Johnson's office before he closes, then pick up the boat. I'll even buy you some Mexican food."

"No way!" That was an ongoing joke between the two of us. As a Texan I refused to eat Mexican food as far north as Michigan. Which is silly, because west Michigan is full of Hispanic-Americans, but I was always sure the restaurants wouldn't serve real Tex-Mex, and I wouldn't touch it.

"German?"

I looked at the work piled up on my desk and thought about my scheduled shift, which was supposed to end at nine-thirty or ten p.m.

Joe spoke again. "Indian? Hungarian? French? Tibetan? Serbo-Croatian?"

I made up my mind. "Three o'clock? I'll be ready. And I vote for Chinese."

At noon Tracy brought me a sandwich to eat at my desk, and I worked straight through until three. Which didn't make up for the time I was taking off, but I did get a few things done. Aunt Nettie doesn't mind if I leave early, but I hate to ask for special treatment.

Joe looked neat—khakis and polo shirt—when he came to get me. I was glad I'd dressed fairly decently that day, since I hadn't had time to go home and change. I got my extra sweater from the van and we started the hour-long drive to Grand Rapids. I was grinning as we drove out of town and got on the interstate.

"You look like the proverbial cat with a mouthful of feathers," Joe said.

"It's skipping out in the middle of the day. I feel as if I'm getting away with something. But tell me what you know about this Tom Johnson."

"All I know about him is that the cashier's check he gave me as earnest money was good."

"A cashier's check is always good, Joe. When are you supposed to finalize the deal?"

"He asked for ninety days. So he's still got a month."

"He didn't tell you what he wanted to do with the property."

"Nope."

"And you didn't ask."

"Nope. I figured it wasn't any of my business. The city has rules about what can go in various zonings. The state has rules about what can go on the lakeshore. It's not my business to enforce their rules. Once that property is off my hands I have no interest in it."

"How did you meet Tom Johnson?"

"He called one day, said Frank Waterloo had mentioned the property to him, and arranged to come down to see it. He'd seen it earlier, of course."

"He told you that?"

"No, but he knew how to find it, and finding it is not that easy. Besides, if I wanted to buy a piece of property, I wouldn't approach a seller until I'd at least driven by it. Though Johnson didn't seem to know where the property lines were, so he hadn't poked around too much."

"Had anybody seen him over there?"

"I didn't ask around. But you know that neighborhood. It's practically deserted until you get to the houses two blocks away. He could have done anything over there."

"Including pulling down the old Root Beer Barrel."

"True. Nobody would have noticed anything. But I am sure he told me he'd heard about the property from Frank Waterloo." Joe reached over and patted my hand. "So, we'll ask him how he knows Frank."

The Root Beer Barrel property wasn't a spot you would simply stumble over while driving through Warner Pier. It was on North Lake Shore Drive—across the river and a couple of miles up the lake from Aunt

Nettie's house. It was located on a section of Lake Shore Drive where Lake Michigan had eaten away part of the road, leaving the structures on the inland side—well, stranded. You had to know how to get there if you wanted to find the area.

Fifty years earlier, I'd been told, that part of Lake Shore Drive had been a state highway. It was lined with motels, service stations, and restaurants. Then the lake had eroded the property on the west side of the road. Several buildings had fallen into the lake. The state highway route was moved several blocks away from the lake, and the businesses on the inland side closed because of the lack of traffic. Yet the spot was still lakefront property. It would be expensive to stabilize the bank, of course, but condos, restaurants—lots of businesses would find the property valuable.

If Tom Johnson had any kind of backing at all, he should be able to redevelop the property successfully.

"Is Johnson expecting us?" I said.

"No. I thought it would be best to surprise him."

"If he's there."

"Oh, he's there. I called. I used what we lawyers call a subterfuge to make sure he'll be there until closing time." Joe glanced over at me. "Now I'm going to ask a sexist question."

"Sexist? You usually seem to avoid that. What's the question?"

"Do you know how to flirt?"

I batted my eyelashes and crossed my knees. "Have I been too straightforward with you?"

"Not with me. I like you just the way you are."

"Then why should I flirt?"

"I've been trying to think about the best way to approach Johnson. He's the kind who isn't even ashamed of being sexist."

"And you want me to vamp him?"

"Not vamp him. I'm not thinking of anything more

serious than getting him to ogle a little. I want to distract him, throw him off balance some way. Have you got a better idea?"

"I don't want to be uncooperative, Joe, but I've tried not to encourage these sexist types. How about if I slap his face?"

"That might be a little extreme. It would be embarrassing if he sued you for assault. We'll have to wing it. But if you think of a way to distract him from the business at hand, just jump in there."

Grand Rapids is a typical American city—all the retail and restaurant chains are there in shopping centers lined up along through streets that can't be told apart from similar streets in Dallas, Miami, Seattle, or, I guess, Boston. In between the shopping centers are the strip malls, and in an older strip development we found the office of Johnson-Phinney Development. It didn't look particularly prosperous.

The outer office was empty, though the reception desk was cluttered with enough debris to indicate that someone usually sat there. As the door closed behind us, a deep voice called from the inside office.

"My girl is out! I'll be there in a moment! Have a seat!"

Joe and I found chairs, and the voice continued talking, apparently on the telephone. It said things like "I'll run that by Phin, but my own feeling is negative" and "Listen, if we don't have the contract within thirty days, the deal is off."

I nudged Joe and pointed to the telephone on the reception desk. It had little plastic buttons for the different lines, and none of them was lighted.

Joe grinned and spoke softly. "He could be using a cell phone." I nodded, but I waited for Johnson with a suspicious attitude.

In a few minutes the telephone call was apparently concluded, and seconds later a big man loomed in the doorway to the inner office. My first thought was

what a perfect Santa Claus he'd make. He was tubby
and had plenty of white hair—lots on top of his head
and even more on his chin. Then he looked at me,
and the Santa illusion faded. Santa Claus doesn't
leer.

His eyes bounced from me to Joe and back to me.
"Helloooo. What can I do for you?"

A creep. I decided he was fair game for flirting. I
lowered my head—he was shorter than I am—and
looked up at him from under my lashes.

"Hi, Tom," Joe said. "Joe Woodyard. We've got a
contract for sale of that lakefront property at Warner Pier."

Tom pulled his eyes back to Joe. He looked blank
for a minute, then grinned broadly. "Joe! Good to see
you. What brings you to Grand Rapids?" He bent
over the reception desk and checked the calendar
there. "I haven't gotten mixed up on the date we
agreed to conclude the property sale, have I?"

"It's still a month off. I just thought I'd check in
with you, see how things are going."

Johnson rubbed his hands together. "Fine, fine! Everything's on schedule!"

Joe shared something interesting that the title
search had turned up, and Johnson topped his story.
Through it all Johnson's eyes switched from Joe to
me and back again. They kept lingering in my direction, but Joe didn't introduce me.

Finally, Johnson gave a little bow. "Now, Joe," he
said. "You haven't introduced me to Mrs. Woodyard."

"My mom?" Joe blinked. "Oh, you mean Lee. I'm
sorry. This is Lee McKinney, Tom. Lee is business
manager for TenHuis Chocolade down at Warner
Pier. She's on the Economic Development Committee
for our Chamber of Commerce."

I'd been wondering just how Joe was going to explain me. I bared my teeth into my Miss Texas contes-
tant smile.

Johnson beamed so widely I expected him to bounce his belly and give a ho-ho-ho. "How d'ya do, Ms. McKinney. Well, well, well. If you're a typical member of the Warner Pier Chamber of Commerce, I guess I'll have to join."

"We always welcome new members, Mr. Johnson." I reached for my Texas accent. "But I will admit I particularly wanted to meet you. Ever'one in Warner Pier is jus'dyin' to know what plans you have for the Root Beer Barrel prope'ty."

Johnson shook his finger at me, looking more like a lecherous Santa than ever. "Now, now, Ms. McKinney, I can't say a word until my funding is fully committed. You must let us developers have our secrets."

"Oh, c'mon, Mr. Johnson. You kin give me a hint." I pronounced it "hee-nt."

He chuckled. "No can do. Not even for a pretty girl."

"We-ell, okay. I'll just have to keep on tryin' to git the information out of Frank Waterloo."

"Who?" Johnson looked completely blank.

Joe jumped in then. "Maybe I misunderstood, Tom. I thought you said Frank Waterloo tipped you off about the availability of the property."

"Oh!" I could almost see Johnson's brain scrambling as he tried to recover. "Well, old Frank doesn't know anything about the specific deal. We just talked about Warner Pier in general."

Joe nodded. "How'd you meet Frank?"

"Damned if I remember. Ran into him at a party someplace. I don't know him well." The Santa smile grew stiff. "Anything more I can do for you two?"

Joe again assured Johnson his visit had merely been a routine call, and I promised to send him some information on the Warner Pier Chamber of Commerce. We all shook hands—he gave mine an unnecessary squeeze—and Joe and I left. Johnson stood in his office window and watched until we were in the pickup and driving away.

"Odd to see a beard with a beard," Joe said.

"What do you mean, a beard?"

"You know, a beard. A front man."

"You think he's acting for someone else."

"It seems likely. Remember that 'Who?' He didn't have the slightest recollection of Frank Waterloo's name. That little session makes me very doubtful that the sale will be concluded."

"Oh, Joe! I hope the deal doesn't fall through."

"I'm beginning to hope it does. On second meeting, I find Charley Johnson on the unsavory side. I'm not sure I want to see him or any of his associates around my home town. Somebody else will buy that property."

"Johnson is certainly not like any developer I ever met before." I shot a glance at Joe. He knew that my past included five years of marriage to a Dallas land developer.

Joe apparently didn't have any qualms about that. "Your ex wasn't so secretive?"

"When he or one of his friends was planning a new project, it was generally hard to get them to shut up about it. Of course, there might be reasons for being secretive. Such as trying to buy up other property in the area."

"I'll ask the other property owners in the neighborhood if they've been approached. But we'd all discussed how much to ask per front foot, and my price was in line with that." Joe hit his turn signal and changed lanes. "Still in the mood for Chinese?"

I used the time it took us to reach the restaurant and get settled in a booth to prepare to bring up the second item I wanted to discuss—my odd conversations with Trey and Meg Corbett.

It was a little early for dinner, so we ordered drinks. After the waiter left, I crossed my knees and did the old-fashioned footsie bit under the table. "How was my flirting?"

"Great!" Joe grinned and used his foot to nudge me back. "Tom never knew what hit him."

"Then let's change the subject. I had a strange talk this morning."

I quickly sketched the conversations I'd had with Trey and with Meg. "It's odd, Joe. I never did figure out what Trey was up to. Was he trying to make me jealous? Was Meg? I didn't understand any of it."

Our drinks came then, and Joe stared at his for a long moment. "Did Meg make you jealous?"

"Not of her. Actually, you have a perfect right to chase any woman you please."

"You're the only woman I want to chase, Lee."

"I'm delighted to hear it. But I don't see you as the kind of guy who chases married women. You're not perfect, but you don't seem to be stupid."

Joe grinned. "I defended a few guys who shot people who were fooling around with their wives. The thought of a husband with a gun sure makes adultery unattractive."

"Do you think Trey has a gun?"

"Probably not. It might wrinkle his pocket protector." Joe stared at his glass again. "I'm not sure what to tell you about Maggie—I mean, Meg. She was Maggie Mae in high school."

"I'm not asking for high school confessions."

"That's a relief."

"We'd all be better off if we could erase our teenage years from our memories. But if you knew Meg back then, or more recently, can you figure out what her motive was in telling me all that stuff about you chasing her?"

"Just trying to make herself appear attractive, I guess. She always thought all the men were after her."

"Were they?"

"Some were. That was one thing that got her talked

about. She was illegitimate, for another thing. And, well—her mother was illegitimate, too. Warner Pier can be a really small town about that sort of thing. My mom's not any more narrow-minded than most, but she really didn't like my dating Meg."

"You were popular in high school, Joe. Class president and wrestling champ. I don't see you taking out the school slut."

"Meg's reputation was nothing like that. She wasn't easy.' She was just a girl who lacked 'background.' Or that's what my mom thought. Meg talked wilder than she acted. I always thought she was dramatizing herself."

"A pretty normal teenage trait."

Joe contemplated his drink seriously, then looked at me. "They say a gentleman never tells, Lee. But as far as Meg went, well, I finally decided she was more of a tease than anything else. If anybody showed an interest in her, she bragged about it."

"That's—well, is 'pitiful' the right word?"

Joe shook his head. "I'm no therapist, but Meg . . . Okay, let's admit it. All us Warner Pier locals look at the summer people with at least a little bit of envy. They have more money than most of us do. They have more status in the larger world. They've *seen* the larger world, and us small-town guys haven't! Some, like Trey's family, are what passes for 'aristocratic' in America. It takes lots of us a few years to get that envy out of our systems."

I knew Joe was talking about himself and his disastrous marriage to a rich and famous summer visitor; her glamor had been one thing that attracted him to her. I'd seen the same feelings displayed by other locals. "Is that why Lindy told me not to date a summer guy if I didn't want to ruin my reputation with the Warner Pier guys?"

"Exactly! That's all based on envy. The Warner Pier guys don't think they can compete, so they bad-mouth

any girl who goes out with a summer visitor. But Meg
broke that taboo. And she got away with it."

"How'd she manage that?"

"She didn't give a hoot about what the local guys
said. The first time she saw she could catch the eye
of a summer guy—and not just as a sexual plaything—
all the Warner Pier guys, including me, were history.

I sipped my drink. "This morning she indicated that
Trey—or Trey's family money and connections—were
exactly what she'd been looking for in life. I wonder
what Trey saw in her."

"A sexy little piece, probably. I hope he wasn't disappointed." Joe lifted his glass. "Here's to Meg. May
she get every damn thing she wants in life, and may
she never bother us again."

"Hear, hear!" I said. "And may we never again talk
about her or about Hershel Perkins or about the
Toadfrog."

And we didn't for at least an hour and a half. We
stuffed ourselves with the deluxe dinner for two—
including Pupu tray. I let Joe worry about paying for
it. Then we drove half an hour across Grand Rapids
to a beautiful neighborhood where an executive of
an office furniture manufacturing company lived. He
proudly showed Joe the boat he'd bought, a twenty-
foot 1955 Chris-Craft Continental. It looked to me as
if it needed a lot of work. His wife made coffee, and
the guy insisted on telling the whole yarn of how he'd
found the boat in an old barn. Joe made admiring
noises, hooked the trailer to his pickup's hitch, and
told the guy he wasn't promising any particular deliv-
ery date.

"It'll take a lot of hand finishing," Joe said.

"I know, I know," the man said. "I've always
dreamed of owning a boat like this. I don't want a
slapdash job."

When we left it was nearly dark. By the time Joe
and I had driven back across Grand Rapids and en-

ered I-196 heading south, there was hardly any light
the western sky.

We were almost back to Warner Pier before the
ext excitement started.

CHOCOLATE CHAT

CACAO CASH

- Cacao was money—literally—to the Aztecs and other Mesoamerican natives. They used the beans as currency, as well as grinding them up and using them to make drinks.

- An early Spanish visitor to what is today Nicaragua reported a rabbit could be purchased for ten beans, a slave for a hundred beans, and a visit to a prostitute for eight to ten beans. Naturally, counterfeiting developed.

- The Aztecs did not weigh cacao beans but measured by counting individual beans. Approximately twenty-four thousand beans would fit in one of the backpacks carried by traders. One early Spanish reporter claimed that the warehouse of the emperor Montezuma held forty thousand such loads, or 960 million cacao beans. Most of these, of course, would have been used for paying soldiers or servants and for buying supplies for the emperor's household, but the household also drank a lot of chocolate.

- On one recorded occasion, when Montezuma was a prisoner of the Spanish, servants of the foreign invaders broke into his storehouses and spent the night making off with thousands and thousands of beans. The beans were stored, it was reported, in huge wicker bins, which were coated with clay.

Chapter 12

L ooking back, we made it easy for the guy.

    One of the disadvantages of living in a quaint and beautiful tourist town, of course, is that a lot of day-to-day items, such as gasoline and groceries, are sold at tourist prices. As Warner Pier business people, Aunt Nettie and I—and Joe, too—try to patronize other local businesses. But when gasoline is a nickel higher per gallon in Warner Pier, some of us are not eager to cough up the difference.

The Marathon station ten miles north of Warner Pier, at the Willard exit, always has gasoline eight to ten cents cheaper than the Warner Pier stations. So Warner Pier locals who've gone to Grand Rapids or Holland universally follow the habit of stopping there to buy gas on their way back into town. As long as we're there, we figure we might as well top off the tank. Besides, the restrooms are usually clean.

Joe hadn't hurried as we left Grand Rapids. First, he's not one of these immature guys who has to pass everything on the highway. Second, he tries to use as little gasoline as possible, though being forced to drive a pickup truck with enough moxie to haul a big boat means he can't worry too much about mileage. Plus,

I-196 traffic is heavy day and night, weekdays and weekends.

Joe didn't even mention his plan to stop for gas. He just pulled off the Interstate at the Willard exit and hauled the boat over to an open gas pump. When I asked him if he wanted a Coke, he said, "I can get them," and I answered, "Oh, I'll do it. If you want a candy bar, you're on your own."

I got out of the truck, visited the ladies' room, then bought two one-liter bottles of soda—one Diet Coke and one regular. As I was going back out to the pickup, I noticed a big black panel truck—the kind a plumber or electrician might drive—parked off to one side. I noticed it for a silly reason. It had tinted windows, and it looked empty, but just when I happened to be looking at it, it moved. It rocked back and forth, just slightly. The motion made me wonder just what was going on inside. I grinned as I got into the pickup and I pointed the panel truck out to Joe when he came back.

He laughed. "I guess I'll have to get my windows tinted," he said. "Turn the pickup into a love nest."

He drove out of the station and onto the entrance ramp, paused until the Interstate traffic cleared, then gunned the pickup until he was up to highway speed. He reached up to adjust his rearview mirror so that it dimmed the headlights of the vehicle behind us. "Jerk's following too close," he said.

I looked back, and I realized the vehicle behind us wasn't only too close. It was coming up really fast, too.

"You'd almost think he was trying to ram us!" I said.

"He'd better not hit that boat," Joe said grimly.

There was no one in the left hand lane, and the vehicle moved out to pass us.

"He could be drunk," I said. "I hope he stays in his own lane while he gets by."

Joe's voice was level. "He's not staying there," he said. "He's coming over. Hang on."

Joe hit the brakes, hard. The boat began to fishtail. Joe edged over to the right, fighting to keep control of the truck and the trailer. I thought we were leaving the road—until I looked out the window. We were on a bridge. The railing was really close. We weren't going to be pulling off on that side. The guy on our left was trying to crush us against the railing.

I took a deep breath and held it. The vehicle kept coming over into our lane. Joe hit the brakes again, whipping the boat back and forth and slowing the pickup.

The speeder missed our front fender by maybe an inch, then shot ahead of us.

Joe touched his accelerator gently, and as we speeded up, the trailer we were towing straightened out.

I exhaled. "Yee-haw! That was close. Good driving!"

"The cell phone's in the glove box," Joe said. "Try to call 9-1-1. We need to report that guy."

I was staring at the vehicle that had just gone around us. It was square in the pickup's headlights and moving away rapidly. I could see that it was a black panel truck. "Is that the truck we saw back at the Willard station?"

"It looks like it. Can you read the tag number?"

"Not the letters." I was reaching into the glove box while I talked. "I think the numbers are eight, eight, four."

The black panel truck was moving away fast, already disappearing around a semi. I found the cell phone and punched in 9-1-1. I spoke as soon as I heard a voice. "We want to report a reckless driver on I-196 just south of the Willard exit. He nearly ran us off the road."

"Where?"

"I-196, maybe a mile south of Willard."

"What state is that in?"

"Michigan!"

"We're Wisconsin."

"Rats," I said. "Joe, the cell phone bounced us across the lake."

"Hang up," Joe said. "We'll call the Warner Pier dispatcher. She can call the state police. We'll try to follow that panel truck, see where the guy goes."

"Sorry," I told the phone. "We'll try a local number."

The semi ahead of us had slowed down, and Joe pulled into the left lane and passed it. He told me the number for Warner Pier City Hall. "How come you have that number memorized?" I said. He didn't answer.

I was punching in the numbers as Joe pulled up beside the semi.

"Where'd he go?" he asked.

The black panel truck had disappeared.

"He can't have been traveling that fast," I said. "He'd have to be driving the speed of light to have disappeared already."

Joe kept his speed up, passing a couple of cars, but nothing that looked remotely like the black panel truck appeared.

"Weird," he said. "I don't think we imagined it." He settled into the right-hand lane and slowed down several car lengths ahead of the cars he had passed.

I was looking back. "Oh, no! Somebody's coming up fast in the left-hand lane."

It was a replay of the whole first episode. The headlights came rushing at us—the driver must have been hitting at least ninety. When the vehicle got beside us, I could see it was the same black panel truck. It was coming over into our lane. And once again the whole thing was happening on a bridge.

"Look out!" I said.

"Hang on!" Joe said.

Again he hit the brakes. Again the boat whipped back and forth, while Joe fought to control the pickup. Again we edged toward the shoulder and slowed.

This time I closed my eyes. When I opened them, the black panel truck was oozing in ahead of us. His tag was right out there in the headlights. Then the truck headed on up the road at warp speed, passing two cars and moving out of our line of sight.

"This time I got the letters from the tag," I said.

I finished calling the Warner Pier dispatcher and told her about the whole episode, including the license plate number. She promised to call the Michigan State Police.

"Scary," Joe said.

"How did he get behind us again? Where did he hide?"

"He must have pulled onto the shoulder, waited until we'd gone by, then taken off again. If we were out beside the semi, we wouldn't have seen him."

"Why? He can't have it in for us particularly."

"I don't know why he would, but he seems to be able to pass anybody else without trying to shove 'em off the road."

"Should we stop?"

Joe thought a minute. "Better not," he said. "We're in danger in the pickup, but if he's really after us, we might be in more serious danger if we aren't moving."

There was no exit from the Interstate before Warner Pier. We drove on. Joe stayed in the right-hand lane. He didn't pass anybody, though the two cars we'd passed now passed us. Joe drove conservatively. But his hands gripped the steering wheel as if it were the neck of the jerk in the black panel truck.

Two miles before the exit to Warner Pier there's a rest area. I've never stopped there—it's too close to home—but I'm sure it's a standard rest area, with

parking for trucks and for cars, restrooms, and ma
chines dispensing soft drinks and snacks. That's where
the black panel truck ambushed us the third time.

We had just pulled past the exit from that rest are
when the semi behind us began to flash its light
and honk.

"What's he doing?" Joe said.

I looked back. "Oh, God, Joe! Here comes tha
panel truck again!"

"He's not going to get away with it this time," Joe
said. He pulled over to the left.

"Joe! There's another bridge! He can push us into
the rail on either side!"

"I've got to try something or he's going to kill us."

The black truck was gaining fast. When he go
within twenty-five feet of us, Joe suddenly moved
right, straddling the center line. Then he hit the
brakes, hard. The boat began to whip back and
forth frantically.

"It's working!" I yelled. "He's dropping back."

Of course, Joe couldn't keep the boat fishtailing. He
had to gain speed or lose control of the pickup. And
of course, as soon as he let up on the brakes and
began to speed up, the panel truck was right on us
again.

Again Joe let him get closer. Again he hit the
brakes, slewing the boat trailer all over the road
Again the panel truck was forced to drop back.

Joe muttered. "That'll never work a third time."

"At least we're off that bridge," I said. "We're
within a half-mile of the exit. Maybe . . ."

"No. Here he comes again!"

This time the panel truck didn't let the boat stop
him. He pulled out onto the left-hand shoulder, appar
ently determined to come up alongside us.

I tried to keep my voice calm. "He's going out to
the left," I said.

Joe fishtailed the boat again, and I felt a shock. "The boat hit him!"

"Not hard enough."

Joe pressed hard on the accelerator, and we pulled ahead. But the black truck wasn't ready to give up. He was even with the pickup's bed now, and he was so close I could see the Dodge hood ornament glittering, could see something shiny inside the cab. Maybe a pair of glasses.

"He's coming over!"

Now Joe suddenly swung the wheel right. The pickup veered across the highway, then off the highway, onto the shoulder. We were racing down the Interstate, but we weren't on the pavement. We were on the shoulder. The black truck shot by us.

Then we weren't on the shoulder any more. We were on the grass. Then we were in the bushes. Then we were heading down a slope. There were trees ahead.

"Hang on," Joe said. The pickup was slowing.

We came to a stop with the hood of the pickup about a foot from a fence post.

Behind us, the semi honked long and hard. He whizzed by.

Joe and I spoke at the same time. "Are you okay?"

Apparently we both were. We unhooked our seatbelts and met in the middle of the pickup's front seat. Neither of us said anything for a long moment. We just held each other.

"Well," I said finally, "if you get tired of repairing boats you can take up driving a race car."

"The finish line didn't go exactly the way I planned. I thought I could stop on the shoulder. But it took a lot longer to brake than I'd expected."

"I thought those trees were going to stop us."

Joe's voice was savage. "The guy better not have damaged that boat."

Joe pulled his flashlight from under the seat and got out to inspect the boat. I started to follow him out the door on the driver's side, but Joe stopped me. "Wait there. There's probably a lot of poison ivy out here, and you've got on that short skirt."

So I sat sideways, with my legs dangling out of the truck. It was a typical west Michigan June night—temperature in the mid-fifties—so I put on my extra sweater. By this time several cars had stopped, and people were coming down the slope to us. We assured them we weren't hurt. I picked up the cell phone, which had landed on the floor, punched "redial" and told the Warner Pier dispatcher what had happened. She promised to have the state police there ASAP.

Joe was dealing with the spectators, so I leaned against the door frame and tried to figure the whole thing out.

What the heck had happened? Three times a guy—or maybe a gal—in a black panel truck had tried to wreck us. The third time he or she had succeeded. Despite Joe's best efforts, we had hit the ditch. Joe's efforts, however, had meant we left the highway gradually and slowed at a suitable rate of speed, and neither of us had been hurt. Our luck had been due, I was convinced, not simply to dumb luck, but to skill on Joe's part and to his experience in hauling boats with that particular pickup.

But why? Why had the person in the black panel truck made such a determined effort to run us off the road? We hadn't seen the truck before we stopped for gas at the Willard exit. In fact, I was convinced I had never seen it before in my life.

Had it been waiting for us?

That thought sent a chill up and down my spine, and I had to admit it was possible. Anybody familiar with the customs of Warner Pier could have predicted we'd stop at Willard on our way back from Grand Rapids. And the truck had been sitting there, waiting.

No one had been visible through the windshield, and the side windows had been so heavily tinted we hadn't been able to see inside them. But, I reminded myself, something had made the truck move slightly. It could have been the driver, moving around inside while he watched us.

Plus, the driver had apparently been familiar with that stretch of highway. At least, he'd known exactly where the bridges were, where being pushed off the road would be most dangerous.

The whole thing was unbelievable. Someone had tried to shove us off the road. Maybe kill us. But why on earth would anybody want to do that?

It was a relief to see flashing red, white, and blue lights on the highway. The state police had arrived.

Once they made sure we weren't hurt, Joe began to describe what had happened. It didn't sound any more logical when he told it than it had when I thought it through. The state police officer, frankly, was looking skeptical.

Just as Joe got to the end of the tale a really tall man walked down the slope. "I lost the S.O.B." he said.

We all stared at him. The state police officer spoke. "Who are you?"

"I was in that semi right behind this guy." He gestured at Joe. "I saw what happened. I tried to follow the jerk who shoved him off the road." He turned to Joe. "You guys okay?"

We assured him we were, and he nodded. "It looked as if you were pulling off slow, and there were other cars around. I figured they'd help you, so I took off after the truck."

Then I remembered that the semi had tried to warn us the last time that the black panel truck attacked. And he'd blasted his horn after we went off the road.

The trucker—he must have been at least six six— said his name was Ron Vidmar. He told us he had followed the black panel truck five miles south, where the truck exited at Haven Road. "I lost him after that," he said. "My rig's not too good as a chase vehicle on those back roads. Lots of houses. Lots of trees and bushes."

"Yeah," Joe said. "There are plenty of summer places down there. Plenty of little roads and subdivisions. But we sure appreciate the effort. Especially since we may need a witness."

I wrote Ron Vidmar's name, address, and cell phone number down and thanked him for coming back to report. A wrecker came. I got out of the truck—refusing Joe's offer of a piggyback ride—walked up to the highway, and stood by the state police car, shivering in the night air, while first the boat and then the pickup were hauled back to the pavement. Joe looked mighty relieved when the pickup started right up.

Ron Vidmar's semi came by again—he'd had to drive back to the previous exit and swing around to get back on the Interstate going the right direction—and he gave a farewell blast of his horn. I got into the truck, and I thought we were on our way when another car with flashing lights pulled off the highway and parked on the shoulder ahead of us. The word "POLICE" was stenciled on its trunk.

Another tall guy got out and walked back to the pickup. Chief Hogan Jones.

"Joe," he said. "What the hell were you doing going to Grand Rapids? Suspects in a murder case are supposed to tell the investigating officer before they take off."

Chapter 13

The state police wanted us off the Interstate, of course, so Chief Jones followed us out to Joe's shop, where Joe opened the double doors at the end and backed the 1955 Chris-Craft Continental inside. He turned on all the lights.

"So why didn't you tell me you were going to Grand Rapids?" the chief asked.

"It didn't occur to me that you'd be interested," Joe said. He began looking at the side of the boat.

"Is it damaged?" I asked.

"A crack and a bad scrape." Joe ran his hand along the side. "That plank had to be replaced anyway. It didn't do anything that can't be fixed."

"Good."

That's when Chief Hogan Jones raised his voice. "You two! Pay attention to me!"

We turned toward him. "I'm sorry, Chief," Joe said. "I guess I'm not thinking too logically yet. Do you want to hear what happened?"

"First, I want to know why you went to Grand Rapids."

Joe and I looked at each other. "I guess it was my fault," I said.

"But it was my idea," Joe said. He sketched our concerns about the old Root Beer Barrel and Frank Waterloo's possible connection to Tom Johnson, who wanted to buy it. Then he told the chief about our trip.

The chief glared. "Then you didn't go to the airport?"

"Why would we go to the airport?" I asked.

Joe and I stared at the chief, and he stared back. I was still mystified, but Joe began to frown. "Who thought we were headed to the airport?" he said.

"He didn't give his name."

"Did you believe him?"

"Not enough to put out an all-points for a blue truck."

"Wait a minute," I said. "Are you saying somebody called you and said Joe and I were headed for the Grand Rapids airport?"

The chief nodded. "An anonymous call. He said Joe was on his way out of the country. Didn't mention you, Lee."

"Why would anybody say that?"

Joe leaned on the boat. "He did it to make it look as if I was fleeing the investigation."

I turned on the chief. "You couldn't believe that! It's obstreperous! I mean, preposterous!"

Joe spoke very quietly. "The chief didn't believe it, Lee. If he had, he would have had the Grand Rapids police pick us up."

The chief looked a little embarrassed. "Well, I did call TenHuis and ask for Lee. Nettie told me the two of you had gone to Grand Rapids to pick up a boat. I figured that if you were breaking for the Canadian border, you wouldn't haul a boat along."

"Certainly not on an airplane," Joe said.

I was still irate. "But who would make a call like that?"

"Apparently I have an enemy," Joe said.

"Yeah," Chief Jones said. "Any ideas on who it might be?"

Joe shook his head. "I guess I've stepped on as many toes as anybody else in my life. But I don't have any idea who would dislike me so much they'd try to frame me for murder. And, Chief, that's what's going on."

The chief nodded, and I decided to jump back into the conversation. "Yeah, and when the chief didn't send the Grand Rapids police after us, whoever this is took direct action and tried to shove us into a bridge railing. Three times!"

I belatedly remembered something about those three episodes, and I turned to the chief. "The license number! I gave the license number to the dispatcher. That'll tell us who was in the black panel truck!"

The chief shook his head. "No such luck, Lee."

"What do you mean? It was a Michigan plate. You should be able to check it."

"We were able to check it. We have a magic computer that checks license plates almost instantaneously."

"What did it say? Who owns that truck?"

The chief sighed. "It isn't that easy, Lee. The license tag number you gave the dispatcher belongs to four-year-old Ford . . ."

"It was a Dodge!"

The chief went on. ". . . a four-year-old Ford pickup. Registered in Dearborn. Sorry, Lee. Either you got the number wrong or the driver of the panel truck faked the tag."

There didn't seem to be a lot more to say or do, so the chief left pretty soon, and Joe began closing up the shop. "Guess I'd better get you back to pick up your van," he said.

"You know," I said, "I may have figured out the real motive of the anonymous caller."

"Yeah?"

"Put your arms around me, and I'll explain it."

Joe complied with my request willingly. A few minutes later he nibbled my ear. "So? Explain."

"Explain what?"

"Explain why the anonymous caller sicced the cops on us."

"It's a part of a plot designed purely and simply to interfere with our romantic life."

"Oh, is that why all this is happening?"

"Yes. Just analyze it. Last night you planned a romantic evening for us. Right?"

"Yep. Boat ride, nice dinner. Even warned you about the possibility of mosquitoes."

"Correct. I'm sure you noticed I wore my sexiest scent of Deep Woods Off."

Joe breathed deeply on the nape of my neck. "Mmmmm."

"And what happens? We barely get dinner down, and we're called back because that dumb green canoe has turned up at the boat shop."

"You just might be right," Joe said. "Just think—later on, after we got everybody cleared out around here, I thought I had enticed you back into the romantic mood and—bingo! Hershel turns up."

"Yes. And that ruined the rest of the evening." I clenched my fists in Joe's shirt. Finding Hershel hadn't really been a joking matter.

"Then today I took up the effort again," Joe said, "luring you up to Grand Rapids. A town simply thick with motels and hotels."

I began to laugh. "Yeah! And think what would have happened if we'd checked into one of them."

"What?"

"The chief would have decided we were taking too long on our trip and called the Grand Rapids police. We would have been hauled out in the middle of our tryst and taken down to the station."

"It might have been worth it," Joe said.

He kissed me again, and this time I didn't laugh. Tears began to run. I had to stop kissing, go into Joe's office, and use one of his Kleenexes to blow my nose. I sat down behind his desk and bawled. He followed me, looking helpless, the way men do when faced with an emotional woman.

"I'm sorry," I said. "This whole thing is just . . . so . . ."

"Yeah. It's getting me down, too." Joe kissed me again, but this time his target was the top of the head. "Come on. I guess I'd better get you back to your van. And then I'm going to follow you home."

"You're the one who's got an enemy."

"Apparently. And the best way to hurt me would be to hurt you."

Aunt Nettie was in bed when I got home. Joe didn't insist on looking in all the closets and under all the beds, though he waited until I was inside. I didn't think I'd sleep, but somehow I did. Pure exhaustion, I guess.

In fact, I slept until after Aunt Nettie had left for the shop the next morning. I had barely dragged out of bed at nine-thirty, when she called the house. "What's this I hear about you and Joe having a wreck?"

"It's a long story. Neither of us was hurt. Who told you about it?"

"Trey Corbett. He came in wanting to know all the details. He apparently had a run-in with the same driver."

That was interesting. Maybe Trey had been able to identify the driver. As soon as Aunt Nettie hung up, I called Trey. I got his chatty answering machine. I left a message, then got ready for work and dashed to the shop.

The ladies in hairnets were bustling about, and Aunt Nettie was standing over her large copper kettle,

the one she uses to make fillings for truffles and bonbons, the one with its own gas burner. The big white
plastic pail of fondant was on the work table next to
her, and as I came in she was using a broad spatula
to dip out a chunk of the fondant and put it onto
a scale.

"Hi, Lee," she said. "I'm sure glad to see you're
not bruised all over." She eyed the scale, then added
the fondant to the copper kettle, adjusted the gas
flame, and began stirring.

"If I'm not black and blue, it's thanks to Joe's driving," I said. "I just wanted to assure you everything
was all right before I went to the post office."

"Fine. But when you get back, I want to hear all
the details."

I gave Aunt Nettie a hug and headed down the
street. The two blocks to the post office and two
blocks back turned into a long walk that morning. It
seemed that every downtown merchant in Warner Pier
had already heard about our excitement and wanted
a personal report.

By the time I got back to TenHuis Chocolade, the
aroma of the place had changed. When I opened the
door I had the sensation that I'd fallen into a vat of
syrup. I realized that Aunt Nettie was making the filling for maple truffles, "A milk chocolate truffle flavored with sweet maple." Sounds like a cliché candy—
I mean, everybody makes a maple cream. But everybody doesn't make one like Aunt Nettie's.

I took a deep breath and walked back to the workroom. Maple flavoring has the strongest aroma of any
flavoring Aunt Nettie uses. Somebody broke a bottle
of it once, and we smelled sickeningly sweet for a
week. But in the proper proportions—in Aunt Nettie's
proportions—maple flavoring smells absolutely wonderful.

I smacked my lips enthusiastically. "Can I lick the
dish?"

Aunt Nettie smiled. She added a ladle of warm milk chocolate to the copper kettle and stirred. "First you tell me about this wreck you and Joe had."

I told her. The whole story. I didn't gloss over what had happened. I gave up trying to keep things from Aunt Nettie a long time ago.

She didn't gloss it over, either. "I don't suppose Joe could take a trip for a while," she said. "Just get out of town and stay away from whoever is after him."

"I don't think the chief would like that. Besides, he would have to come back eventually."

"And Joe doesn't have any idea who would be so eager to get him involved in Hershel's death?"

"No. The whole thing won't be resolved until the chief catches the person who really murdered Hershel. Right now, it strikes me that the best way to do that would be to find out who was driving that black panel truck."

Aunt Nettie vigorously stirred the mixture in her copper kettle. She added the maple flavoring. "Trey said he'd call back. Maybe he saw something."

It was an hour before I heard from Trey. He came in the door, looking more nerdy than ever. He seemed scrawnier. I wondered if he was losing weight, though he didn't have any to lose. I motioned for him to come into the office.

"You okay?" I said. "Aunt Nettie said you had a run-in with the same jerk Joe and I did."

"The chief says it sounds like the same truck," Trey said. "Black Dodge Cargo Van. At least I think it was black. I'm guessing by the color of the paint down the side of my Explorer."

"It actually hit you? I didn't realize that. What happened?"

"I'd been over to Gray Gables—you know I'm the local caretaker for the family?"

I nodded. "It's a beautiful place. Do they ever have tours?"

"No, but I can show you and Joe over it. My cousins don't come down much. Anyway, last night I left there a little after ten, and I decided to head back to town on Inland Road, rather than getting on the Interstate."

"I didn't realize Gray Gables was that far from town. I've only seen it from the water."

"It's not far, but the roads over there are so twisty it's quicker to go down Haven Road, get on the Interstate, and come back that way."

"Haven Road! That's where the black panel truck got off the Interstate."

"Apparently so. I had just turned onto Inland when this black vehicle came up behind me, traveling like the proverbial bat out of hell. He went around to pass and scraped along the left-hand side of my Explorer. I'm just darn lucky I didn't have my arm out the window. I nearly ran off in the ditch. Then I blasted the horn—I'm sure everybody in the neighborhood heard me. Of course, he didn't stop."

"Did you see where he went?"

"He turned off to the left, but I couldn't see just where. Michigan Road. Lakeview. Maybe even Benson Drive."

"Are there other houses around there?"

"Oh, yes. It's a built-up neighborhood. But the lots are big."

"I wonder if anybody else saw him."

"Chief Jones was going to ask. He was also going to try to find out if anybody in that neighborhood owns a black Dodge Cargo Van with tinted windows."

"Did you get a look at the license plate?"

"I thought you and Joe got the number."

"We thought we did, too, but when they ran a check, the number we had was not the number of a Dodge panel truck."

Trey frowned. "I thought it had a couple of eights. I guess they could have been sixes. I didn't get the letters."

I gave Trey a sample chocolate—he picked a milk chocolate fish on a stick. Then I walked outside with him to see the damage to his silver SUV. An awful scrape ran down the driver's side, and the black paint showed up clearly.

"This guy must be crazy," I said.

"The chief's convinced he had it in for Joe. He thinks I just got in the way. Does Joe have any idea what he did to annoy him?"

"No."

"I don't know Joe all that well. It seemed to me he usually tries to mind his own business. I never heard of him making anybody mad. Of course, there was that Chicago man who wanted to make an offer on the Ripley place. Joe wouldn't even talk to him. I guess that guy was kind of upset."

"Someone wanted to buy the Ripley place?"

Trey got a look of little boy guilt on his face. "Joe didn't tell you? Maybe I was wrong." He shuffled his feet uneasily. "Guess I'd better go. I'm supposed to meet a painter. I'm still working on the Miller cottage."

He left, repeating his offer of a tour of Gray Gables. I went into the office with something new to think about.

Somebody had offered to buy the Ripley place? That sounded completely screwy.

The Ripley property, also known as Warner Point, was the showplace home of Joe's ex-wife, the famous defense attorney Clementine Ripley. It included a fabulous house on a ten-acre plot which was bounded by Lake Michigan on the west and the Warner River on the south. The property was part of the estate which had become such a booger for Joe to settle. The Ripley property was worth millions, and it was costing her estate thousands in upkeep.

Clementine Ripley might have been a brilliant defense attorney—the one movie stars and politicians called when they were in trouble—but she hadn't been a good financial manager. She'd also owned a co-op apartment in Chicago, and she and Joe had owned an apartment house jointly. All of her real estate, Joe said, was heavily mortgaged. Plus, she'd trusted the wrong person with her finances, and nearly every cash asset and almost all her investments had been stolen or transferred to offshore accounts that were not in her name. She hadn't even gotten around to signing a new will after she and Joe were divorced, which was the reason he was stuck with settling up. Getting any of the stolen assets back was proving to be a legal nightmare.

And thanks to the current drop in the real estate market, Joe had told me, he didn't want to sell the Chicago real estate. The co-op apartment was rented. The apartment house made a profit, but it also kept Joe's personal savings tied up. Between them, the two pieces of property provided barely enough income to pay the taxes, insurance, mortgage payments, and maintenance on the Warner Pier estate. No one wanted to rent the Warner Point property—which might have something to do with the two murders that had occurred there, I guess. It was simply a money pit and a pain in Joe's neck financially.

If I was reading the situation right, Joe ought to be glad to sell the Ripley property. So, if he had a chance, why wouldn't he have sold it?

I could call him up and ask him, of course. But I'd been so careful to stay out of his financial affairs, I didn't quite have the nerve. If Joe wanted me to know, he would have told me.

Probably, I told myself, the offer hadn't been enough to pay off the mortgage.

For a minute I wondered just what my future with Joe was. We'd never discussed marriage. We'd never even explored those important questions like "Do you want to have kids?" and "Do you want to live in

Warner Pier forever?" These things just hadn't come up. So how could I quiz him about his finances? They weren't any of my business, as things stood.

The phone rang, and I sighed and reached for it. I'd better quit brooding on company time.

That phone call was the first of many. A dozen people called that morning—Joe's mom, making sure I was all right; our neighbors, the Baileys; the chair of the chamber's Economic Development Committee; lots of others. It was a replay of my walk to the post office.

"I might as well have stayed home," I said as Aunt Nettie walked by the office door. "I can't get a thing done for the telephone."

Aunt Nettie smiled. "I'm glad you're here. If you weren't, I couldn't get a thing done for the telephone."

The morning passed. It was straight up noon when the twelfth call came. "Lee! Are you okay?"

It was Lindy Herrera, who had been a friend since we were teenagers.

"Hi, Lindy. Yes, I'm all right. Joe's all right. Even the truck's all right."

"You don't sound all right."

"I'm just tired, I guess. The phone's been ringing off the desk, and you're the first caller I actually wanted to talk to."

Lindy laughed. "Sounds as if you need to do lunch."

"Not in Warner Pier. It'll be just like taking the phone with me. Are you working today?" Lindy worked in the restaurants and catering business of her father-in-law, Warner Pier's mayor, Mike Herrera.

"Actually, I'm a lady of leisure this summer. I decided to stay home with the kids. But today they've gone to the Grand Rapids Zoo with my mom and dad. Why don't you come out here? I'll fix something."

An idea began to tickle my brain. "Isn't there a park up Inland Road, not far from Gray Gables?"

"Riverside Park. Why? Are you in the mood for a picnic?"

"Yes, I am. And maybe a drive around that neighborhood with a local guide."

"You're on. I'll fix the sandwiches."

"I'll bring chocolate."

Chapter 14

Warner Pier is, as I say, a small town. And one sign that a town is really small is that everybody is related to everybody else in some way. If they're not blood relations, they go to the same church, went to high school together, get their hair cut at the same shop. It's a mishmash of interconnected circles.

For example, back when Lindy Herrera was Lindy Bradford, she and I had worked together behind the counter at TenHuis Chocolade for three summers. At eighteen she married Tony Herrera, who had been a close friend of Joe's in high school. Tony's dad, Mike Herrera, was now Warner Pier mayor. He owned three restaurants and a catering service, and he also dated Joe's mom, Mercy Woodyard, who ran Warner Pier's largest insurance agency, with offices right across the street from TenHuis Chocolade. Interconnected circles.

The circles continue. Tony has a job as a machinist in Holland, but when he was laid off the previous summer, he worked for Joe. Lindy works for her father-in-law. Since she fills in the gaps where Mike needs help, I never know if I'll see her dishing out barbecued chicken at the Chamber of Commerce banquet or serving up French dips at Mike's Sidewalk Café, a half-block from TenHuis. Our circles intersect all the time.

Tony and Lindy have three kids. Tony works days and Lindy usually works nights. I know they have trouble making ends meet. It was the kind of life my parents had, until debt and the struggle to get by drove them apart. It was the kind of life I had been trying to avoid when I scrambled my way through college. But Lindy and Tony seemed to be coping.

I picked Lindy up at her little house at Ninth Avenue and Cider Alley. "I brought Cokes and chips," I said. "And I hope you still like strawberry truffles."

"Yum, yum!" Lindy held up a small Styrofoam cooler. "I've got turkey wraps and carrot sticks. This is quite an outing for me. No kids!"

"Your kids are darling."

"Of course they are. What would you expect? But school's barely out, and I'm already frazzled."

I tried not to think about the fact that I was twenty-nine years old and had no kids and no prospect of having any. We crossed the river on the Orchard Street bridge, then turned on Inland. We passed the Waterloos' house, which still had a driveway full of cars.

"I guess I've seen Riverside Park from the water," I said. "But the main thing I remember about it is a boat ramp."

"For years a boat ramp really was the only thing there," Lindy said. "In the last few years the city's fixed it up—playground equipment, a picnic shelter. I think the land was given by the Corbett family. Years ago."

"Does it adjoin Gray Gables?"

"It doesn't adjoin, but I think the Corbetts owned acres and acres on that side of the river originally. Now there's a whole housing addition between the park and the big house."

We pulled into the park and easily found a space to spread the old quilt I keep in the back of the van. Several boat trailers were parked in the proper places for boat trailers, but picnickers were few. Yet the park was very nice—shady, with a well-kept playground.

"Is this park a secret from tourists?" I said.

"I think they all go for the beach. I bring the kids over here sometimes. Now, how about this tour you mentioned?"

"It's just idle curiosity," I said. While I ate my turkey wrap—it had special horseradish sauce I remembered paying extra for at Mike's Sidewalk Café—I described the adventures Joe and I had had with the black panel truck. Then I added Trey's experience.

"So the truck disappeared out in this area," I said. "That doesn't mean it's still here, of course."

"It could have hidden out a while, then gotten back on the interstate or taken off by the back roads."

"Sure. So I don't want to go door-to-door or anything. That's Chief Jones's job. But I realized that I've never been over here enough to have any idea of what's here or how it's laid out."

Lindy laughed. "I think I can find my way around. Tony and I parked on every road on this side of the river."

"It'll have to be a short tour. I do need to get back to the shop."

"Okay. But now I gotta know. Has Joe proposed?"

I should have expected that, I guess. But, Lindy caught me by surprise, so I stumbled around. "We haven't been dainty—I mean, dating! We haven't been dating but four moons—I mean, months!"

"Four months! More like a year."

"We met each other a year ago, Lindy. We didn't date for a long time after that."

"Well, you ought to . . ."

"Lindy!" She stopped talking and looked at me expectantly.

"Neither Joe nor I wants to make another mistake. Don't rush us!"

I said that merely to shut Lindy up, but when I heard my own words, they convinced me. For the moment at least, I felt confident about my relationship with Joe. It was unsettled, but so what? I didn't know where it was going. That was fine. I said as much to Lindy. "It's okay."

Lindy shrugged. "Okay."

"So, what's going on with you?"

The most exciting development in Lindy's life, to my surprise, was her job.

"Mike wants me to start working for him full-time in the fall," she said. "I'll be a sort of second-in-command for the catering business."

"That sounds like a promotion."

"At least it's a raise. I'll be meeting clients, deciding on menus, stuff like that—very little cooking and serving. It won't mean as much night work, since somebody else will handle the actual events. So maybe Tony and I will get to see each other now and then."

"Sounds good."

"Mike has a sense of family, you know. He couldn't get Tony interested in the business, so he's turned to me."

She gave me a full report on each of the kids, and I told her about my mom—who's a travel agent in Dallas and is frequently off to Timbuktu or Tanzania. Then we hashed over the romance between her father-in-law and Joe's mom, a topic I don't discuss with just anyone—particularly not Joe.

After we got that settled Lindy began to stuff paper napkins and other debris into a plastic sack. "Are you ready for the tour?"

"Sure. I want to see all the romantic spots where you and Tony made out."

Driving on up Inland Road brought us into an area

that had as many trees as the road up to the old chapel had. It wasn't scary in the daylight, with the sunlight making patterns on the forest floor here and there, but the trees were thick and crowded the road.

There were quite a few houses, but the woods made most of them feel secluded. "This is Riverside Addition," Lindy said. "It was a hot development when I was a kid. My mom used to wish she could afford to move over here."

"There are some beautiful homes—when you can see them."

We wandered around on several side roads, including the ones Trey had mentioned: Michigan, Lakeview, Benson Drive. They were lined with houses, but all the houses were heavily landscaped. Bushes, shrubs, and big trees were everywhere.

"This is like driving through the deep, dark woods," I said. "Only now and then a house peeks out."

"It's a lot like your aunt's neighborhood."

"I know, but her house was built a hundred years ago, when that area was rural. The houses over there 'just growed.' This neighborhood actually encouraged all these trees. None of these houses get any sun. Not a woman over here can see more than three feet out her kitchen window."

Lindy laughed. "A little further along here, the road ends at the entrance to Gray Gables. You can turn around there."

In a quarter of a mile the road curved, and I found the hood of my van up against an elaborate iron gate, closed and locked, with iron fence stretching out on either side. Beyond it, a gravel drive led into a small grove of trees. I caught a glimpse of a roof—a shingle-covered cone—high above the trees.

"Trey offered to give Joe and me a tour of this place," I said.

"You should see it," Lindy said. "The Corbetts

have lent it out a few times for special events I served, but it's hard to get inside. It's fabulous. Like going back in time. All the original furnishings."

"I think I'll take a closer peek, as long as we're here."

We both got out of the van and walked up close to the gate. I craned my neck to see around the darn trees. "I can see one corner," I said. "Queen Anne modified. Gee! It matches the side you can see from the river."

Lindy laughed. "If you can identify the style of the house by seeing one corner, you've been hanging around with the artsy-fartsy crowd too much."

All I could see of the house was the tower that held up the cone-shaped roof. The bottom two floors were clapboard and the sides of the tower's top floor were shingled. It was all, of course, painted gray.

"I wonder why they put the observation tower on the inland side of the house," I said.

"It's on the lake side."

I turned around and looked behind me. "Lindy, Gray Gables is on the river, not the lake. The lake is nowhere near here."

"Look at a map, Lee. It's only about half a mile. When this house was built, or so I've been told, you could see the lake from the house."

"Unbelievable! I told you all these trees would cause problems. It would have been fabulous to be able to see the river on one side and the lake on the other. But no more. Not that this isn't a lovely spot."

Lindy took a deep breath. "And one of the loveliest things about it is the smell," she said. "Just like Ten-Huis Chocolade."

For a moment I thought I must smell like maple flavoring. Then I sniffed and caught the same odor Lindy had identified. "It *is* chocolate," I said. "Where do you suppose it's coming from?"

"It can't be from Gray Gables. That's too far away."

We looked around. No sign of human habitation. Except . . .

"Lindy! There's a house over there."

I pointed. Among the trees to our right I had caught sight of tell-tale evidence. A straight line, running diagonally among the tree branches. Straight lines are never found in nature.

"Oh, my gosh!" Lindy said. "There is a house. And it's real close—right behind that row of trees. But there's no drive."

I pointed to a narrow gap in the bushes. "I guess that's a path."

"But how would you get to the house in a car?"

At that moment the bushes burst asunder and a giant stepped out. "The drive comes in from that road on the right!" a voice roared. "It's wide enough for my VW!"

Lindy and I actually clutched each other. I was nearly as startled as I had been when Hershel popped up outside the window of Joe's truck. "Yikes!" I said. "Where'd you come from?"

The giant—now I realized it was a giantess—laughed. It was a deep, rolling laugh, a laugh that matched her appearance. I'm very close to six feet tall, and this woman towered over me. She must have been at least six foot three. And she was broad. I would guess her weight at well over two hundred pounds; she had a bosom like the prow of a battleship. And after the first shock of her size, her coloring was equally shocking. Her hair was a bright red, and her face was ruddy and freckled. Her eyes bugged, and they were bright blue. She was wearing blue jeans and an enormous, brilliant blue sweatshirt with the name of an Ann Arbor restaurant across the front.

"Didn't mean to startle you!" she roared. "I'm staying in the cottage for the summer! Heard a car stop! Stepped out to see what was going on!"

"We were gawking at Gray Gables," I said. "I'm sorry if we disturbed you."

The giantess laughed again. "Ho! Ho! Ho! Not at all!"

Lindy was peeking through the trees behind the woman. "Did you say you're staying out here? Isn't it awfully remote?"

"That's what I like about it!" The woman didn't seem to be able to speak at a normal sound level. Every sentence was shouted out. "Wanted to get away from people for a couple of months! Cabin's pretty ramshackle, but it has electricity! Walk to beach! Only low-rent place I could find!"

She looked at me and her expression grew even more jovial. "Hey! You work in that chocolate shop. I can tell by your shirt!"

"Yes." It was hard not to yell back at her. "I'm the business manager, Lee McKinney. Have you been in?"

"Naturally. Ms. TenHuis gave me a tour!"

"Oh, Aunt Nettie mentioned it. You're the friend of Mrs. Corbett."

"Yes! Not a close friend, but she rented the cottage to me. I loved your shop! Chocolate! That's my kind of flesh-pots!"

"Be sure you come back." I walked toward the woman, with Lindy trailing along. Our reason for being there belatedly reappeared in my tiny brain. "I suppose the police have already bothered you today."

"Police! Ho, ho, ho! Do I look like a crook?"

"Not at all. They're investigating an accident I was involved in last night." I sketched our reasons for wanting to know if the black panel truck had been seen in the area.

"Doubt he'd come up this road. Dead end!"

"Right. Unless the driver was a stranger. So you didn't hear anything?"

"Not last night. Two nights ago was the commotion!"

"I doubt that had anything to do with our accident. But what happened?"

The giantess gestured over her shoulder with a thumb. "Back in the woods! Closer to the Interstate! Hobo jungle!"

"Oh!" Lindy gasped. "I'd be terrified if I was out here alone."

The red-haired woman gave a shrug, and her whole body shook as if she'd been hit by an earthquake. "They don't bother me. I don't bother them."

"Except two nights ago," I said. "You said you heard a commotion."

"They didn't bother me! I just heard them. Thrashing around in the woods. Yelling!"

"Oh." I decided the woman knew nothing about the black panel truck. But she was sure an interesting character and apparently a TenHuis customer. "Let me give you a card," I said. "Next time you come in the shop, we'll have an extra sample for you."

I got my purse out of the van and wrote "Quarter pound box" on the back of a business card. Then I gave it to the giantess.

She read my name, then offered her hand in shaking position. "I'm Dolly Jolly!"

I remembered that Aunt Nettie had said she had a funny name. My opinion must have showed, because Ms. Jolly spoke again. "Dorothea, of course! But I've always been Dolly!"

"Like Dolley Madison. One of my heroines."

She beamed. "Love chocolate!"

"You must be baking," I said. "We smelled cookies."

"Chocolate chip. I'm writing a cookbook!"

"Then you're a real foodie. So's Lindy." I introduced them and included Lindy's job. "I'm just a bookkeeper. And I've got to get back to work."

We got in the van and started to drive away, but after I'd turned around Dolly Jolly waved us down again. She came up to my open window and spoke.

"Another fellow might have seen your panel truck! Prowls around everywhere! By here nearly every day the first week I moved in! Little guy with dark hair and a big mouth! Raspy voice! Looks like a frog!"

CHOCOALATE CHAT

CHOCOLATE—RICH AND RICHELIEU

- By the early 1600s, the Spanish royal court was drinking chocolate—probably using recipes for a hot beverage which the Spanish occupiers of Mexico had sent home.

- Chocolate requires quite a bit of processing—fermenting, drying, winnowing, grinding—so it's not surprising that working people rarely drank it, either in the New World or the Old World. It was not only expensive to buy, but expensive to prepare. Only the richest Spanish could afford it.

- Tradition has it that when the Spanish princess Anne of Austria was married to Louis XIII of France, she brought chocolate along as part of her dowry. However, Anne—she's the one whose troubles Alexandre Dumas described in *The Three Musketeers* was only fourteen when she married and apparently never had much influence over her bridegroom. Other authorities believe that chocolate was introduced to France by the Cardinal of Lyon, who then passed its secrets on to his younger brother. Since that younger brother was Cardinal Richelieu, also a character in *The Three Musketeers* and a guy with more clout than anybody else in seventeenth century France, chocolate was soon popular.

- Another report states that nuns in a Mexican convent produced delicacies of solid chocolate quite early. And they apparently made good money selling these in Europe. The Sisters of St. Godiva?

Chapter 15

"Hershel!" Lindy and I spoke at the same time.

"That his name? Figured everybody in town would know him! He lectured me about the little cabin. Said it was a workman's cottage from the 1850s. Kind of a character!"

"We won't be asking Hershel anything," I said. "He was killed. Night before last."

I told Dolly about finding Hershel's body.

"Rotten deal!"

"It was pretty awful," I said.

"Hershel? That his name? Over here Monday! Close to dark!"

"Monday? That's the night he disappeared!"

Dolly scratched her head. "Think that was it. He walked out of the woods. I was sitting out, enjoying the twilight!"

"You ought to tell the police chief about this."

Dolly shrugged. "Don't know anything! Didn't tell me he was going to get killed!"

"I know the chief is trying to trace his movements Monday night."

I wrote the chief's name and the location of the police department on the back of another TenHuis

:ard and gave it to her. We offered her a lift to town,
>ut Ms. Jolly said she would call the chief for an
ıppointment.

"Got a cell phone!" she shouted. "Won't bother to
;et a landline connected! Don't need the Internet! I'll
ake my VW to town!"

We left then. After we reached Haven Road, Lindy
>egan to laugh. "I hope that VW's a van," she said.
"That's the largest woman I've ever seen."

"Not too many people of either sex make me feel
daalinty," I said. "But she did. And think of her seeing
Hershel the night he disappeared."

I drove a few blocks before I spoke again. "I wonder what Hershel was doing out by Gray Gables?"

"I can't imagine," Lindy said. "Trey Corbett
might know."

I decided I'd had enough contact with Trey for one
day, but I did plan to give Chief Jones a call instead
and tip him off about Dolly Jolly. But when I got back
to the office, work intervened. All afternoon I actually
had to earn my salary. Customers called wanting rush
orders sent out. Our sugar supplier had our bill
screwed up, and I had to talk fast, dig out two months'
bank statements, find copies of canceled checks, and
fax the copies to them before the crisis was settled.
Barbara, a close friend who's manager of the Warner
Pier branch bank, dropped by—apparently making a
customer call—and stayed. And stayed. And stayed.

Barbara is an attractive brunette of maybe forty.
She has a business degree from Kalamazoo College.
She has big dark eyes and a nose so large it dominates
her face. Barbara doesn't care about her nose, and
after her customers see her smile, they don't either.
She's as smart as a tree full of owls, as my Texas
grandma would have said, and she's got a real head
for figures. She's been a valuable friend and colleague
to me since I moved to Warner Pier, but that afternoon I thought she'd never leave.

Barbara had finally headed for the door when she dropped a small bombshell. "I guess Frank and Patsy Waterloo may put their divorce on hold," she said.

"Divorce! The Waterloos? I hadn't heard that."

"I heard it from one of the high school teachers. Not at the bank. Loose lips sink banks. So it's just gossip."

She left then, but she left me curious. Just what was the story on Frank and Patsy Waterloo? Why would Hershel's death affect any plans they had for a divorce one way or another?

I knew who probably knew the answer to that, but I sure hated to sink low enough to ask him. I was glad when the phone rang and distracted me. "TenHuis Chocolade."

"Lee? Hogan Jones here."

"Oh! I was thinking about calling you, but I never found time. Lindy and I ran into this woman . . ."

"Big redhead."

"Yes. Dolly Jolly. I guess she came in to make a statement."

"Right. She says she told the two of you that Hershel was out at Gray Gables the night he disappeared. Have you passed that information on to anybody?"

"No."

"Don't. Okay?"

"Whatever you say. But why not?"

I could hear the chief sigh. "She saw more than she realizes. If it gets out—she could be at risk."

"Oh!"

"I know you wouldn't want to be responsible if anything happened to her."

"Of course not! I won't say a word. Do you want me to call Lindy and tell her to keep quiet?"

"I'll do that. Don't talk about it to anybody, okay? Not Lindy. Not Joe. Not even Nettie."

I hung up feeling cowed. What could Dolly Jolly

have seen? It took me twenty minutes to calm my curiosity down. Until the next time the phone rang. It was Joe.

"Did I talk to you about going out to dinner tonight?" he said.

"I don't think so."

"Well, I can't get away."

I laughed. "Gee, Joe, when you start breaking dates we hadn't even made . . ."

"Pretty much of a jerk, huh. I meant to ask you, but the telephone repairman says he'll be coming around five. I guess I'd better not plan on any particular schedule."

"How about me bringing a pizza out there?"

"Hey! That sounds like a pretty good deal."

We agreed that I'd come at my own convenience. I discussed the dinner break schedule with Stacy and Tracy, and about five-thirty I called the Dock Street Pizza Parlor and ordered. Then I decided to pick up a bag of salad at the Superette on the way. It would be cheaper than the Dock Street's salad.

Or that's what I told myself. The truth, of course, was that I was still curious about the Waterloos, and the person most likely to have wormed out the real story on them was to be found at the Superette—Greg Glossop, who ran the pharmacy there. If "Mr. Gossip" didn't know the real story—well, he'd make up something interesting.

As I'd anticipated, all I had to do was walk into the drug and beauty supply end of the Superette and look at a display of mascara. Greg Glossop bounced his little round belly right out of his glassed-in pharmacy. He trotted down the nearest aisle and greeted me. "Lee!"

"Oh, hello, Greg," I said.

"Well, young woman. You've had a nasty experience."

"Finding Hershel, you mean? It wasn't a lot of fun Of course, we weren't really friends. It's Patsy and Frank I feel sorry for."

"Tch, tch," Greg said. "Of course, we've all fel sorry for them all along."

"Taking care of Hershel must have been an awfu strain." I leaned a little closer and lowered my voice "I even heard that they were considering divorce."

Greg Glossop nodded wisely. "I guess the whole situation was really getting Frank down. Between the responsibility for Hershel, Frank's problems finding a good job, and their money situation—it would get any body down."

"Patsy seemed sincerely sorrowful about Hershel' death, but I could understand if it was something o a relief. Maybe that will solve one of the problems."

"It'll solve two. It's no secret that Patsy and Her shel's mom left her whole estate in trust to take care of Hershel."

"Oh, really? That's odd. But I guess she figured tha Patsy and Frank could take care of themselves."

"Exactly. And Hershel couldn't. But that mean Patsy and Frank had to move back to Warner Pier which meant that Frank had to quit his job and take one that apparently pays a lot less."

"Of course the house they inherited is worth a lot."

Greg Glossop shook his head. "They didn't inheri it. The property belongs to the trust set up to care for Hershel."

"You mean they were dependent on Hershel?"

"No, no. Just for use of the house. But the trust requires that all of Patsy's mother's money must sup port Hershel. Now that Hershel's gone, Patsy get the trust."

"Did the trust pay when they renovated the house?"

"No. I hear they used the money from the sale o

their California house for that—and apparently they didn't have a lot of equity. Anyway, I'm under the impression that rebuilding the house here nearly wiped them out."

He leaned closer and lowered his voice. "It's understandable if Frank got so frustrated he—well . . ."— Glossop cleared his throat—"went a little crazy. Didn't come home nights. Began to hit the bottle."

That was news. I lowered my voice. "Oh?"

"I'm merely guessing by his purchases in the liquor department. And from some of Patsy's remarks."

All of a sudden I felt as if I'd fallen in a mud hole. And I was so ashamed of myself that I probably blushed. I could barely pay Greg Glossop off with a tidbit about one of the ladies who worked at TenHuis being pregnant. She was telling everybody, so I wasn't letting any cats out of any bags. Then I sidled toward the produce aisle, and Greg Glossop had to leave me and go back to his eyrie above the drug and beauty department.

I picked up my bag of salad and stood in line at the checkout stand, feeling ashamed of gossiping. But I was also looking at another possible motive for getting rid of Hershel. A motive for Patsy and Frank. Not only was Hershel an annoying and frustrating relative to have on their hands, he'd also forced them into a bad financial position and threatened their marriage. And if Frank was fooling around or drinking— I didn't consider Greg Glossop's evidence conclusive; Frank might have been taking booze home to Patsy— Hershel's spying might have inconvenienced him, as well.

Yes, Frank and Patsy were going to be a lot better off without their troublesome relative—financially and personally.

I picked up the pizza and headed for Joe's. When I got there, the telephone company's truck was parked beside the shop and the shop's doors were all open, but there was nobody around. I called out, but nobody answered.

I decided that Joe and the repairman were probably tracking down the phone problem. I took the salad and pizza and went into Joe's little cubbyhole of a bedroom-living room-dining room. He'd already set the card table with plates, forks, knives and a can of parmesan cheese, but he hadn't anticipated salad. I found a couple of bowls in the cupboard and filled them with salad.

Still no Joe. I decided that the microwave oven was the only small, enclosed space in the room—the only place where the pizza might stay warm. I had just clicked the microwave's door open when I heard a noise in the shop, and Joe came to the door.

"Hi," I said. "Dinner's just about ready."

"Will it wait? I want you to see something."

I put the pizza in the microwave, then followed Joe outside. He led me down the drive and out onto the road—actually the tag end of Dock Street, but that far from the center of town, it had turned into a gravel road.

"What are we going to see?" I asked.

"The phone man found it. I've called the police."

I stopped dead. "Not another body!"

"No! I wouldn't drag you out to see something gruesome."

I continued to follow Joe, but with some dread. A line of utility poles, of course, followed the road. Wires were over our heads, mixed in among the trees. In about a hundred feet I saw a man in the uniform of the phone company.

"I want you to show that wire to Ms. McKinney," Joe said.

Wordlessly, the phone man pointed down. A cable trailed down from above him, and the end lay near his feet.

The end. It wasn't attached to anything. The other end led up into the trees. But this end was just lying on the ground.

The phone man looked almost pleased. "It sure wasn't equipment failure," he said. "This wire was deliberately cut."

Chapter 16

Chief Jones arrived shortly. Joe and I left him taking pictures and went back to the shop to eat our salad and pizza. When I drove away a half-hour later the telephone man was up on the pole, and the chief was walking toward the shop. We waved at each other.

An hour after that the chief showed up at Ten-Huis Chocolade.

I was in my office, working away, when I saw him come in the street door. He paused and peered around the shop, looking more Lincolnesque than usual. Tracy and Stacy were busy with a half-dozen tourists, so I waved, and the chief came on back. He slouched down in a chair. Somehow ordinary furniture never seemed tall enough to fit Chief Jones.

"What happened to the phone line?" I asked.

"Somebody cut it."

"Somebody climbed the pole and cut it?"

"I didn't say that. I don't know exactly how the guy did it. He could have brought a ladder or climbed on top of a truck or swung from a tree like Tarzan. Me, if I wanted to cut a phone line, I'd use a pruning hook. The kind on an extended pole."

I sighed. "Not too hard to find in orchard country."

"Nope. Matter of fact, Joe's nearest neighbor has one, and he keeps it in an unlocked garage. But now I want to ask you a couple of questions."

"Sure. But I don't know a thing about that phone line except that Joe's phone wasn't working on Tuesday. And finding it was cut would seem to be yet one more factor proving that Joe is innocent. He's definitely the victim of a frame-up."

"I didn't come to talk about Joe. I want you to go over what Hershel said to you when he came up to the truck that night."

I collected my thoughts a minute, then retold the episode. Hershel, after scaring me half to death, had demanded to meet Aunt Nettie at the old chapel. He had refused my offer to get medical help. He had refused my assurances that people missed him and were looking for him. He had refused to trust anybody but Aunt Nettie.

"I don't want to hurt your feelings, Chief," I said, "but he particularly scoffed at you, Trey, Jerry Cherry, Meg, Patsy, and Frank. He said, 'I saw that bunch on the dock.' "

"Don't forget, Joe was there with us."

"I admit that. And we all know Hershel was already mad at Joe. But he was quite firm about not trusting any of you. Talked as if he suspected some sort of conspiracy."

"He didn't go into details?"

"No. I was surprised when he included Trey. Apparently they'd become buddies during the remodeling of Patsy and Frank's house."

"I think Trey had been real patient with Hershel while he was working on the Waterloos' house, but Meg didn't share his patience. Hershel started hanging out at Trey's office and at their house. Meg finally called me to complain about Hershel. Trey backed her up, of course. Hershel couldn't understand that he had to."

"He had to back up his wife, you mean?" The chief nodded, and I went on. "Patsy said Meg complained that Hershel was stalking her. But Patsy said he wasn't really interested in Meg. She thinks it was just Hershel's fascination with Trey."

"I think that was a lot of it, but we have to remember that Meg can be pretty fascinating by herself."

Was I imagining it, or was the chief giving me a sidelong look? "If you meant that for me personally," I said, "I'm aware that Joe and Meg dated each other in high school. I talked to Joe about it, and he doesn't seem to be harboring a guilty passion for her. Does all this seem to fit into Hershel's conspiracy theory?"

"I don't see how. But you're forgetting me. Apparently Hershel suspected me of conspiring against him."

"He also seemed to suspect Jerry Cherry."

The chief grimaced. "I can't find that Jerry ever had any particular contact with Hershel. Hershel may have mistrusted his uniform."

I grinned. "I trust you both, Chief."

"Thanks. But I admit I got crossways with Hershel over the way he roamed around town. A couple of times we had window-peeping complaints about him. I had to be the bad guy."

"It sounds as if Hershel wasn't as harmless as Patsy thinks."

"Oh, he just looked. And a warning would stop Hershel. If I told him, 'Don't go around the Corbetts' house again,' he might grumble, but I could feel sure he wasn't going to go over there. Patsy says I scared him after Meg complained, but Hershel didn't act scared when I talked to him."

"That's funny. Patsy said he hid. That she found him trembling all over. If you didn't scare him, what did?"

"Maybe I'd better try to find out. But now I want

to ask you a different question. Who'd you tell that you were going to Grand Rapids last night?"

"Aunt Nettie."

"Who else?"

"Nobody, Chief. I was a little embarrassed about leaving early, so I didn't tell the girls on the counter I was going on a date. Aunt Nettie may have told somebody."

But when we asked Aunt Nettie, she denied mentioning it to anybody. "It just didn't arise," she said firmly. "Besides, it's nobody's business but Lee and Joe's."

Bless her heart, she'd been avoiding gossip.

The chief asked her several ways. Had she talked on the phone about it? Had Joe's mom popped in and brought it up? Had anybody come in asking for Lee and she'd said, 'Oh, she's gone to Grand Rapids'?"

Aunt Nettie denied every situation. "I didn't mention it to anybody," she said. "In fact, I went home right after Lee left. I left Hazel and the counter girls in charge. But I don't think any of them knew where Lee and Joe had gone."

"We didn't mean for our trip to be a secret," I said. "Joe may have told someone."

The chief shook his head. "He says he didn't. We know nobody called him—his landline was out of commission, and apparently you and his mom are the only two people who ever call on the cell phone. And he says his mother didn't call yesterday afternoon." He turned to me. "You see why it matters?"

I nodded. "If someone called you and said we were headed for the Grand Rapids airport . . . And if that panel truck lay in wait for us at the Willard station . . ."

"Right. Our boy had to know you were coming."

On that happy note the chief went out the door, leaving my innards all atremble. I'd already faced the possibility that somebody had deliberately tried to shove us into a bridge railing—three times. The whole situation was scary. Could that be connected with Hershel's death? I didn't see how.

But to me Hershel's murder had almost become a side issue. Whoever had killed Hershel also seemed determined to implicate Joe. That's what worried me.

Somebody had to know Joe and I were going to Grand Rapids. And nobody had known.

I suddenly realized I was partially wrong. No one had known we were going to Grand Rapids, but one person had definitely known we were there.

Tom Johnson.

Tom Johnson, who looked like Santa Claus and leered like a satyr. Tom Johnson, whom Joe had described as "a beard," a person who's acting for someone else. He had talked to us at his office and would undoubtedly have realized we were likely to eat dinner before we headed back. Tom Johnson, who had signed an option to buy the old Root Beer Barrel property.

We were right back to that lot. I didn't understand why. But I did know I wanted to talk to Joe. I was reaching for the phone when it rang.

"TenHuis Chocolade."

"Lee? It's Joe."

"I was just going to call you."

"What about?"

"The chief was in asking who I'd told we were going to Grand Rapids. I hadn't told anybody. But someone knew we were there."

"Yeah. Tom Johnson."

"Did you tell the chief that?"

"No. I admit I didn't think of him at all until a few minutes ago. When Tom called me."

"He called! What did he want?"

"He wants to finalize the deal on the Root Beer Barrel property next week."

"Whoops! I guess your suspicions were wrong, Joe. I guess ol' Tom really does want to buy the property."

"Ol' Tom or his pal, whoever that is."

"You still think he's acting for someone else?"

"Oh, yeah. But I guess that's not my concern. I'm getting the money I wanted for it. I haven't had a chance to check with the other property owners along there, to see if they've had offers."

"You could still back out."

"I'd owe him some interest on his earnest money, but I guess Clem's estate could find the bucks somewhere. I'll ask around before we close the deal. And I know a few guys in Grand Rapids. I'll try to find out if he has any connection with some other developer."

"I was wondering if he had any connection with somebody who owns a black panel truck."

"I'll leave that one up to Chief Jones. But I'd sure hate to queer the sale of that property merely because of my suspicious nature. And speaking of that property—how'd you like to go by there tonight? After you get off work."

"I won't be off until nine-thirty or ten."

"I know. The moon is just visible over the trees now. Nine-thirty or ten ought to be a good time for a boat ride."

"Well . . ."

"And the lake's supposed to be calm. Wind five miles per hour from the southwest."

I laughed. "In that case, I'll meet you at the dock."

Joe had known the prospect of a calm lake would be the final enticement. I love being out on Lake Michigan—particularly in the moonlight—but rough water gives my tummy trouble. A moonlight cruise isn't romantic if one party is leaning over the side of the boat. It's lucky Joe's love of boats emphasizes working on them and admiring them. If he wanted to go places in them all the time, he'd ditch me and my queasy innards in a hurry.

Anyway, I called home and warned Aunt Nettie that I'd be late. Joe appeared at the door of TenHuis Chocolade at 9:31 P.M. He swept the floor while I balanced the cash register and Tracy and Stacy alternately giggled and cleaned the counter and the showcases. I got my jacket and scarf out of the van, and we were all out of the shop by 9:50 P.M.

The temperature was brisk—mid-50s. But Joe was right about the moon; it was full and gorgeous. He had brought the Shepherd Sedan, and the motor gurgled soothingly as we puttered down the river channel through the no-wake zone that led clear out to the lake. The motor meant there was no conversation, but what did we need to say? We were alone. Everything was beautiful, and I don't mean just the moonlight, the lights of the houses and businesses along the shore, the ranks of boats in the marinas. Then we passed the jetty that protected the river channel as it emptied into the lake, and the water unfolded before us, stretching to the horizon to the south, to the north, and to the west. The moon had moved into the western sky, and its reflection created a path to infinity. I felt as if we could turn the boat onto that path and follow it right up into the stratosphere. We did not need a rocket ship; we had the Shepherd Sedan.

Joe didn't turn into the moon's path, of course. He turned right, swinging out beyond the sand bar that parallels the shore, and we headed north, about a quarter of a mile offshore. We passed Warner Point and the elegant mansion which was giving Joe such fits as he tried to settle his ex-wife's estate. Neither of us even pointed at it. Then we saw the trees and the houses along North Lake Shore Drive, with rolling, tree-covered dunes behind them. In the moonlight, the private stairways leading down to the beach were clearly visible, as was the one block of condominiums that had been built on the lakeshore. Far ahead, miles away, we could see the warning beacon from the lighthouse at Holland. It was all like a dream, and we both were in a sort of reverie as the boat gurgled along in the brilliant moonlight.

We weren't completely alone out there. There were other boats. Most of them were farther out. Many were big—some people would be sleeping out there, others would be fishing, there might be a party going on aboard one of the yachts. But none of them was close to us; no one seemed to be interested in us as we moved up the lake.

After the block of condominiums, the shoreline was marked by a section of trees. When we were opposite that spot, Joe cut the engine. His required running lights and his anchor lights were on, but the brilliant moonlight almost hid them. The boat swayed gently. Calm is a relative term when it comes to a giant body of water like Lake Michigan. The lake isn't like an ocean, but it's never really still. Warm water was rippling gently up from Chicago, a hundred miles away.

I gave a huge sigh. "If you could bottle the peace and quiet out here and sell it, we could retire tomorrow."

Joe chuckled. "And people think I was stupid to quit practicing law so I could fool around with boats." He pointed at the shore. "Can you see the Root Beer Barrel site?"

"What is there to see, now that it's collapsed?"

"I always find it by the old DeBoer house."

"I can't see a thing."

"Here." Joe took my hand and pulled me to my feet. We went to the back of the boat, out from under the sedan's roof. He put his arm around me, took my right hand in his and used my finger to point toward the shore. "Now do you see it?"

"Yes. If it's that tall sucker with all the turrets."

"Right. It's a huge place. Three stories high, plus attics. After that section of Lake Shore Drive went commercial—back in the 30s, I guess—they tried every kind of business in that house. Boarding house, tourist home, restaurant. The ambulance service was there for a while. It's been empty for ten years now, and it's in bad shape."

"But still on the historic list."

"All of Warner Pier is a historic district, remember."

I nodded. "I'd never even noticed the—what did you call it?"

"The DeBoer house. No relation to the diamond people. The house sits to the north of the Root Beer Barrel property, but it's back from the street and those trees you dislike so much hide it. You can't see anything of it except the roof, and you can only see that from the water." He swung my pointing finger to the south. "On the right-hand side of the Barrel is the Old English Motel."

"That I've noticed. In fact, it always seems familiar to me."

"I think there were a lot of motels built on that pattern at one time, fake English cottages, tiny motel rooms with pointed tile roofs. You've probably seen one somewhere else."

"I guess that's it. There's one very similar to it in my home town."

"Dallas?"

"My real home town. Prairie Creek, Texas. Home to cowboys for 150 years."

"You gotta take me down there some day."

I turned around and put my arms around Joe. He put his arms around me. The moment became quite romantic.

Until the spotlight hit us.

We jumped apart. The boat rocked madly, and I grabbed the roof to keep my balance.

"Dadgum!" I said. "Is one of those boats court-busting?"

"Court-busting? What's that?"

"That's what my dad calls driving up and down country roads shining a bright light into parked cars."

"I don't think that's what these people have in mind," Joe said. "They're coming right at us."

The light was growing closer, and the boat's motor was getting louder. I had the impression that it was a big boat, too, at least twice as long as the sedan. I couldn't see clearly because of the light.

I realized Joe had ducked back under the sedan's roof and slid behind the wheel. He looked back at me and yelled. "Get down!"

I ducked back under the roof and into the seat on the passenger's side. The sedan's motor burbled into life, and we began to move forward. I was dying to ask Joe if he thought we were about to be boarded by pirates, but I couldn't. The boat was too noisy. But the situation seemed ridiculous.

Joe gunned the motor, and we jumped forward. The sedan isn't the fastest boat on the lake, but it can move pretty well. And Joe moved it. We headed up the lake, parallel to the shore, at top speed.

Joe used his thumb to gesture over his shoulder. I deduced that he wanted me to keep an eye on the bigger boat.

It was easy to see. It had that spotlight aimed right at us. And the spotlight kept coming closer. It was following us.

Chapter 17

"Closer! It's closer!" I screamed the words, but I knew Joe couldn't hear me.

He seemed to understand. At least he began what I would consider evasive action. He cut the sedan's lights, all of them, even the safety lights. He swung hard left. The searchlight lost us, then found us again. He swung right. The same thing happened. The light lost us, then found us again. Then Joe repeated the maneuver—left out of the spotlight, then—after it focused on us again—right, into the dark.

All the time he was doing this, the big boat was getting closer. The sedan is a great boat, but it isn't particularly fast. I knew that eventually the larger, more powerful boat would be able to catch us. Dodging in and out of its searchlight wasn't going to be a useful escape technique in the end.

And it could well be the end. If the bigger boat hit us—I pushed the mental picture of flying debris and flying bodies out of my mind.

I crawled back to the rear seating area and lifted the seat, revealing the hatch where the life jackets were stored. Right at the moment, a life jacket seemed like a really good idea.

The boat swerved again, and I was thrown sideways. But this time Joe didn't straighten out. We kept traveling in a circle. Centrifugal force almost glued me where I'd landed, against the side of the boat. But we were out of that damn searchlight.

I struggled to get up, at least to my knees, and I finally made it. The sedan was bouncing over the waves—I was just grateful that they weren't very big waves. I looked up and saw the bigger boat going by—I could see oblong portholes, chrome railings, and a big area of smooth and shiny white fiberglass.

The sedan straightened out then, and I looked around Joe to see where we were going. There was nothing but lake ahead; the big boat was behind us. Joe had made a U-turn, and we were headed in the opposite direction, south instead of north, toward the Warner Pier channel.

I allowed myself to hope that we'd make it.

But the big boat was turning, too. Already it was broadside to us. As I realized that, Joe suddenly cut the sedan's speed drastically. The boat settled back in the water like a duck landing on a pond, and we were moving at no-wake zone speed.

"What are you doing?" I yelled. "We were getting away."

Now Joe turned the boat again, heading it directly toward the shore, which was about a quarter of a mile away. He inched along, the motor gurgling gently.

I put my lips close to his ear. "What are you doing?"

"Trying to hit the channel!"

I looked ahead. The only channel I knew of was the channel of the Warner River, the channel we'd come out of. It was marked with lights. I could see it—still far south of us.

I stayed on my knees. Maybe prayer would help. I sure didn't understand what Joe was doing.

But I understood what the big boat was doing. It

was turning in circles, casting its searchlight all around, trying to find us. When it did, it was going to come at us like gangbusters. And instead of racing down the lake while we had the chance, we were moseying along. A kid with an inflated sea serpent and a good flutter kick could have passed us.

Just then the sedan shuddered, and Joe threw the motor into reverse. We inched backward. Then he changed gears again and we inched forward. We moved a few feet, then the boat shuddered again. Joe threw the motor into reverse again. We inched backward, but this time the boat shuddered and stopped moving almost immediately.

Joe turned the motor off. He turned sideways in his seat and began to pull his shoes off.

"We're aground," he said. "Shuck your shoes and your jacket. And those slacks. We're gonna have to swim for it."

"Swim! He'll run us down in the water!"

"We'll be inside the sandbar, and he'll be outside. I think it's our best chance."

I reached for the locker that held the lifejackets.

"We better leave the life jackets," Joe said. "Or better still . . ."

He snatched two life jackets from me, stood up, and hurled them out into the lake, away from the shore.

"Maybe those'll distract him for a minute. And if he does know how to get around the sandbar—and there is a way—they'd make us too easy to spot." He planted a quick kiss on the top of my head. "I think I remember enough about being a life guard that I can get us ashore."

"I can swim," I said.

"That'll be a help."

I pulled my jacket off. Then I yanked off my tennis shoes without untying the laces. I looked up to see a pair of blue boxer shorts in my face—Joe and I were undressing in close quarters and he'd just dropped his jeans.

"Keep that scarf on," Joe said. "That blond hair would be easy to spot in the water."

"I'm keeping my shirt, too. If I drown, I don't want my body to be found in nothing but a padded bra."

Joe was climbing over the side by that time, and he just stood there, with his head and shoulders visible. I peeled my khaki slacks down. "Is it that shallow?"

"We're on the sandbar. Come on!"

Right at that moment the search light hit the water about thirty feet from us, and if I had any tendency to hesitate, I lost it. I tumbled over the side like a skin diver, with my slacks still around my ankles.

The west Michigan theory is that a southwest wind brings warm but dirty water to the beaches. A north wind brings cold but clean water. Or so swimmers are told. After that night, I'll never believe that again. The wind and waves might have been moving in from the southwest, but the water was so cold that Lake Michigan might as well have the Antarctic Ocean. My tumble over the side paralyzed me.

Joe grabbed me and got me to my feet. I gasped and regained the ability to move. We both ducked down behind the boat. I finished stepping out of my slacks.

"Ready?" Joe said.

The searchlight's beam bounced off the boat. "Ready," I said. I took a deep breath, did a surface dive, and pulled hard in the direction of the shore.

I came up about twenty-five feet away. Now my feet couldn't touch the bottom.

"Lee! Lee!" Joe's voice sounded frantic.

"Come on!" I said. "I'm heading for shore!"

I struck off, using the breast stroke with some idea of not splashing. Joe caught up with me shortly. "You said you could swim," he said. "You didn't mention diving."

After that we didn't talk a lot. We stayed close together, and once Joe suggested that I stop and float for a minute. I must have been panting. He was panting, I remember that. He turned onto his back and pulled me over, so that I was lying on my back on top of him. We both concentrated on floating and breathing easily for a few minutes. Funny how hard something like breathing can get. Swimming may be like riding a bicycle, in the sense that you never forget how, but I was way out of condition. And a quarter of a mile is several laps of an Olympic-sized pool.

About half the time we were swimming that big boat was circling around behind us, but it didn't move closer to shore, so I thought it was staying out beyond the sandbar. Once the searchlight cut the water quite close to us, and light seemed to be headed in our direction.

"Sink," Joe said.

I held my nose and sank. I stayed under as long as my lungs held out, and when I popped to the surface again the light was nowhere to be seen.

I'd stopped looking toward the shore because it seemed so far away. But finally I peeked, and this time the tree line was looming almost over my head. I put my feet down and felt the rounded stones of Lake Michigan.

"Maybe I'll walk the rest of the way," I said.

"It's gonna be mighty cold when we get out," Joe said.

The water was up to my armpits. We waded across ten feet of stones, then sand began. We came out of the water on a narrow beach about thirty feet from a creek. Trees grew up the bank, which towered above us. I would have sunk down and rested, but Joe yanked me along, toward a set of stairs that led up the bank.

"I don't want to stop while we're in the moonlight,"

he said. "Besides, we're going to get even colder when we quit moving."

I knew he was right, though I was about played out. We kept going, across the beach and up the stairway. When we got to the top, I did stop.

"Joe! This is somebody's backyard."

"Right. Maybe they left a beach towel on the porch."

"Maybe they'll call Aunt Nettie to come and get us."

Joe nodded.

But the house was dark, and there was no beach towel on the porch.

My teeth were chattering. "Sh-sh-should we b-b-break in?"

"I'm not sure I can manage to burgle a house barefoot and in my skivvies. Let's go around in front, see if we can spot a light somewhere. We may even know somebody in this neighborhood. Once we figure out where we are."

I checked my watch and discovered it was still running. "You'd think some of these people would want to stay up to watch the eleven o'clock news," I said. "There ought to be a light someplace."

We made our way around the house—trampling a flower bed in the process—and found ourselves out on what had to be Lake Shore Drive. Suddenly I recognized a landmark. "Joe! That big tree! The one almost out in the middle of the road. I know that tree!"

"Yeah. We're at the back of Clem's place."

"I don't suppose there's a security guard there."

"No, but I can get in."

Hand in hand, almost naked, soaking wet, and shivering in the fifty-degree temperature, we headed toward the Ripley place, the one that was giving Joe such fits as he tried to settle Clementine Ripley's estate. I'd become acutely aware that my wet T-shirt didn't cover my underwear. I wasn't willing for everybody in Warner Pier to be sure I was a natural blond, so I wrapped my scarf around my waist like a pareo, and it clung to me like a sheet of ice. But the hardest part of the deal was my feet. I kept stumbling over rocks, and I'll swear there was more gravel than blacktop on that road.

"I think I'm leaving bloody footprints," I said.

"Just keep leaving them."

We persevered, though I cast longing glances as we passed a couple of houses with lights. But Joe seemed eager for us to reach the Ripley place before we asked for help. After about five minutes of pussyfooting down the road we came to the big gate that marked the entrance to the estate.

Joe went to the key pad next to the gate. I shivered and my teeth chattered. Down the road, I saw lights reflected off the trees.

"Here comes a car," I said. "Maybe they'll help us." I stepped toward the street.

Joe grabbed my arm and pulled me back into the bushes. "Let's make sure they're not looking for us," he said.

We waited until the car had gone slowly by. I hated to see it go; it had represented help. I sighed. "I guess I probably wouldn't stop if I were driving down a lonely street and a couple of naked people jumped out of the bushes at me."

Joe didn't answer. He just pushed buttons on the key pad, and the gate to the Ripley estate slid open. Then we had another long walk up a blacktop driveway. This one was completely shaded by trees, so we had only intermittent patches of moonlight to see by. Gravel had been scattered on it, too, and had landed in the most unlikely places. My feet hurt so bad I almost forgot how cold I was.

We had to go clear around the house to reach the key pad that opened the back door. Once we were nside Joe hit the light switch, and I saw that we were n the back hall, with the kitchen beyond.

"Whew!" I found a kitchen stool, sat on it and ubbed my feet. Joe went straight to the telephone. He found the directory on a shelf under the phone, earched for a number and punched it in. "Mike? Is Mom there? It's important."

A pause. "Hi, Mom. Lee and I were out in the edan, and we had a little excitement. We wound up aving to abandon ship and swim ashore."

I heard squawking noises from the telephone.

"We're okay! We're okay! Lee's a good swimmer." oe turned and grinned at me. "We came ashore not ar from Clem's place, so we came in there. But we eed clothes and shoes. Can you get something from ny place and bring it out here? There's a key behind he downspout."

More squawking. Then Joe looked at me. "What izc shoe do you wear?"

"Nobody's feet are as big as mine. Tell her not to vorry about shoes. My feet are beyond help already."

Joe repeated what I'd said. "But hurry, Mom. Okay? I left the sedan aground, and I want to go et it."

Joe hung up, then immediately looked for another umber. "Harry? Hope I didn't get you up."

I realized he was calling Harry Barnes. Harry ran a narina in Warner Pier.

Joe quickly sketched our problem—but I noticed he adn't told either his mother or Harry how we got in his fix.

"I left the Shepherd Sedan aground," Joe said. "I ant to get it off quick."

He listened, then spoke. "I was trying to hit the ittle channel that runs out from North Creek. But it's oo narrow this year."

He paused. "Harry, you can laugh all you want ater. Right now I need two favors."

Harry's voice echoed on the phone. "Yeah, yeah. I'll tell you about it later. But I need you to give me a tow. And on your way, see if that Tiara 5200 of Jack Sheldon's is docked."

He was silent. "Just see if it's in its slot! I'll meet you at the Ripley boathouse, okay?"

He hung up.

"Joe, I hadn't thought about the sedan. I do hope it's not damaged."

"It's not as likely to be damaged as it would have been if we hadn't abandoned ship." He put his arms around me. "You're not damaged. That's the main thing."

We hugged each other, but it didn't help us warm up much. Joe said the heating system had been turned off, but he found an electric heater in the pantry and plugged it in. I looked through the kitchen drawers, and all I found were some dishtowels. Joe draped one around his fanny like a sarong, and it hit me that he was feeling as naked as I was. Wet boxers are pretty revealing.

One other thing had me puzzled. "Joe," I said, "I assume you think that this boat you mentioned is the one that chased us."

"I'm not sure. It looked like a Tiara 5200, and Sheldon's the only guy who docks a boat like that in Warner Pier. It could have come up from Saugatuck or down from Holland."

"Or South Haven or Chicago or Onekema or Milwaukee or Sheboygan. But you didn't tell either your mom or Harry that it chased us."

Joe frowned. "I don't want to get held up making statements. I want to look at Sheldon's Tiara and get the sedan off the sand bar. Then I'll tell Hogan Jones what happened."

We were just beginning to get warm when a buzzer rang.

"That'll be Mom," Joe said.

He went to a control panel and spoke into it. "Yes?"

"Let us in." It was Mike Hererra's voice.

"Come around to the kitchen." Joe punched a button.

"I guess I should have known Mike would come with her," I said.

When Mike's car came around the side of the house a second car followed. And this one had lights on top.

"Damn," Joe muttered. "The chief's with them, too."

Mercy jumped right out and ran to Joe, making mother noises. Joe assured her he was all right, but his eyes didn't leave the chief's car.

Chief Jones unfolded himself and got out of his car, then walked over to us. He shook his head slowly, almost sorrowfully. "Well, Joe," he said, "I never had a heck of a lot of success with women back in my young days, but I will say I never had to run a boat aground to get one to go skinny-dipping with me."

Chapter 18

Joe's prediction came true, of course. The chief wanted to hear the whole story. Harry's boat was honking down at the Ripley place's boathouse and Joe was still wrapped in a dishtowel and arguing with the chief.

"Joe!" I said finally. "Take the chief with you!"

My suggestion apparently had merit, because the two of them ran off toward the boat. Joe carried an armful of clothes, and he had stuffed his feet into a pair of sneakers. He looked so weird that Mercy, Mike, and I stood there and laughed until after he and the chief were out of sight.

Mercy had brought me some sweatpants and a sweatshirt of Joe's. Plus, bless her heart, a pair of his white socks and some sandals.

"Not very glamorous," she said, "but they'll get you home without freezing. I didn't want to take time to go by my place and try to figure out something better."

"They look gorgeous," I said. "I doubt you own anything that would reach past my knees. Not being able to borrow clothes is one of the problems of being nearly six feet tall. On the other hand, none of my high school friends ever wanted to bolster—I mean, borrow!—they never wanted to borrow my clothes."

Mercy turned her back and spoke very casually. "I looked for some underwear for you, but I couldn't find anything."

Gee. Even my boyfriend's mother thought I might be keeping clothes at his place. I answered in what I hoped was the same casual tone. "My underpants are nearly dry, and with this sweatshirt I can go braless."

I put on the sweatpants and shirt in the powder room off the back hall. When I came out Mercy made some efforts at asking me just what had happened, and I told her, in a general way. I didn't understand everything, of course. I wouldn't have recognized the boat that chased us, for example. I could only describe it as having one of those chrome railings all around the front, the kind that look as if they're designed for people to walk around on the prow when the boat is traveling a hundred miles an hour.

"Tall," I said. "It loomed up over us. And fast. A lot faster than the sedan."

I guess I shuddered, because Mike Herrera gave me a one-armed hug. "Mercy," he said. "Let's get this young lady home."

They took me back to TenHuis Chocolade, where I picked up my van, and for the second night in a row, I was followed home by someone worried about my safety. Mike and Mercy even insisted on coming inside to make sure no one was lying in wait for me. Naturally, Aunt Nettie heard our whispers and got up, so Mike wound up searching the entire house before we could persuade him to leave. He even called the police dispatcher and, using his authority as mayor, directed her to have the patrol officer on duty drive by the house periodically. He seemed a little let down to learn that Chief Jones had already given that instruction.

He did pick up one piece of information. Jack Sheldon's Tiara 5200 had been found tied up at one of the public docks in the Dock Street Park. The night patrol officer had gotten Sheldon out of bed, and Sheldon had denied having the boat out that evening. He also admitted he kept a key to the boat on a nail in his garage. When he checked, the key was gone.

Oddly enough, Sheldon lived across the street from Frank and Patsy Waterloo. Hmmm. I wondered if that was significant, or simply another of the interconnecting circles of small town life.

Aunt Nettie was twittering, but I was so tired I couldn't make sense of what she was twittering about. I crawled up to bed and slept until eleven a.m. There's nothing like vigorous exercise to ensure a good night's sleep.

I woke up sore in every muscle—another effect of vigorous exercise. I lay in my bed, a mahogany number once occupied by my grandparents, and stared at the ceiling. As soon as I remembered the reason I hurt all over, I began to try to figure out why I'd been forced to go swimming in a cold lake and to walk down gravel-strewn roads in even colder night air, barefoot and in my underwear.

Someone had chased Joe and me in a boat—much the same way they had chased us in a truck the night before. Who? Why?

It kept coming back to the Root Beer Barrel property. Hershel had argued with Joe about it, had become so angry he actually tried to hit Joe. The next thing we knew, Hershel was dead, and somebody was trying to make it look as if Joe had killed him.

But there were intermediate steps. First, we still didn't know who the guy in the black panel truck was, and we didn't know how he had found out we were on the road back from Grand Rapids so that he could lie in wait for us. I resolved to ask the chief if he'd been able to find out if Tom Johnson had phoned anybody in Warner Pier after we left him Wednesday night.

Second, how had the creep in the boat known we were going to be out on the lake?

Now, that was a real stumper. He could have followed us, but it didn't seem likely. Following people is not all that easy in a town the size of Warner Pier—especially around Joe's shop, which was almost in a rural area. A tail would be hard to miss. He would have had to hide some place, see Joe leave in the sedan, guess that he was picking me up, steal the Sheldons' key, steal the Sheldons' boat, and beat us out into the lake.

It would have been a lot easier if he'd known where we were going and waited for us. But we'd only decided to go an hour before we left. I hadn't told anybody where we were going, and I was sure Joe hadn't either. We'd made all our plans on the telephone.

I sat up, even if it did hurt. Well, duh! The answer was as plain as a Hershey bar without almonds. Joe's phone was tapped.

I tried to jump out of bed, and every muscle rebelled. This made me slow down in my rush for the telephone, and I realized I couldn't call Joe to tell him his phone was tapped. In fact, it might be that my phone was tapped, too, so I didn't want to try his cell phone. I threw on some clothes—my own, not Joe's—and headed for the boat shop.

I was let down to see the Michigan State Police mobile crime lab van outside.

I jumped out of my van and limped into the shop. Joe met me at the office door. "Have they found the bug?" I said.

He nodded. "You figured that out, huh? Have you figured out who put it there?"

"No. Have you?"

"Nope."

"There's no way to tell by looking?"

"Today's taps don't have to use wires. They have little transmitters. You can order them on the Internet. Guy wants to check on his tap, he parks a mile away and dials it up."

"Anyway, that tap absolutely proves that somebody's been trying to frame you. Though I don't understand why he also cut the phone line."

"All I can figure out is that he wanted me to be unreachable at that specific time. So he cut the line. But once the line was repaired, he wanted to listen in."

"And then he tried to kill you."

"I'm not so sure about that, Lee. Seems as if every time somebody tries to hurt me, you're along."

I stared. "That's silly! No one would want to kill me."

"Why would they want to kill me?"

"I don't have a specific reason, but it's got to be something to do with the old Root Beer Barrel. Mixed in with hate. Malice. Envy. Avarice. One of those seven deadly sin deals."

"Why would none of those apply to you?"

I found a chair and sat down. "I'm just too darn lovable, I guess." Then I looked up at Joe. "I don't think I'm important enough for anybody to dislike that much. But I don't see why anybody would dislike you either."

Joe pulled up a second office chair and sat down beside me. He took my hand. "You are darn lovable, Lee. And you try to get along with people. I don't see why anybody would want to kill you. But all this has got to link up with Hershel's death. Is there anything you haven't told the chief about what Hershel said? When he came up to the truck?"

"No! The chief asked me about that in detail yesterday, and I went over the whole conversation. I did not hold back a thing. Besides, no one else was there

o hear what Hershel had to say. If he told me who
illed him—right out loud—what's the difference?
he murderer has no way of knowing. Unless your
ickup is bugged."

We sighed and stared for at least a full minute. Then
oe spoke. "I'm sure of one thing. The guy is work-
ng alone."

"Why?" I said.

"Because if there'd been two people in Sheldon's
oat last night, we wouldn't be here now. If there'd
een one guy to operate the light, and a second one
o handle the boat—well, we'd never have been able
o get away. They would have run us down."

That vision of shattered mahogany planks flying
hrough the air—and Joe and me flying with them—
ounced through my mind. I resolutely shoved it back
nto my subconscious. "He—or she—may also have
een operating an unfamiliar boat," I said, "since it
was stolen."

Joe nodded. "In fact, I don't think he—or she—was
used to a boat that size at all. Something about the
way it swerved. But I can tell you another thing. Whoever chased us gets around Warner Pier a lot."

"Why do you say that?"

"He—or she—knew about the old chapel and that
Hershel hung out there. He—or she—knew where to
get the keys to Sheldon's boat. He—or she—knew
how to disappear down Haven Road. He knew where
o find a black panel truck."

"You don't think the guy owns a black panel
ruck?"

Joe shook his head. "No. This baby is too smart to
use his own boat or his own vehicle when he's up to
no good."

"It's got to be somebody close to Hershel, Joe."

We both thought. I spoke first. "My money's on
Frank."

"Why?"

I sketched what I'd learned from Barbara and from Greg Glossop.

"Hardly conclusive," Joe said. "And Frank hasn't lived in Warner Pier very long."

"Five years!"

"Has it been that long?"

"Long enough for a lot of Sunday drives. He's a neighbor to the Sheldons. And he and Patsy are sure better off without Hershel."

"To an outsider it seems that way. But Patsy doesn't seem to think so. Speaking of the Waterloos—are you going to the funeral?"

"When is it?"

"This afternoon. I guess I'd better stay away. The chief thinks Patsy might hit me with a spray of chrysanthemums."

"I'll check with Aunt Nettie and find out the proper Warner Pier etiquette."

I reached for Joe's phone, but he pushed my hand aside. "Use my cell phone."

I could feel my eyes getting round. "Is the phone still bugged?"

"The chief is considering leaving it that way. So don't say anything about it, okay?"

I didn't have time to think about that. I called Aunt Nettie and was instructed to be ready for Hershel Perkins' funeral at one p.m. "Your light blue dress will be fine," she said. "Or something similar."

"I remember," I said. "Don't wear more black than the widow. In this case, the sister."

I hung up. "Gotta go. My hair's still full of Lake Michigan ick." I started for the door, then turned back. "I didn't ask about the sedan. Was it damaged?"

"No. Harry and I got it off the sandbar before the waves pushed it around enough to do any damage. Oh, I've got your clothes." Joe brought a bundle out of his room. "At least, here are your shoes and your jacket."

"I guess we can write off my socks and khakis. Darn
! Those pants were new."

Joe looked stricken. "I'll walk that stretch of beach.
Maybe they'll wash ashore."

"Never mind. I'm not sure I'd want to wear them
again."

By one o'clock I had clean hair and was wearing a
longish black and white print skirt, a short-sleeved
white cotton sweater, and flat-heeled black pumps.
Patsy and Frank had decided on a graveside service
for Hershel. About twenty-five people gathered in the
Warner Pier Cemetery—I recognized the corps of high
school teachers, plus some people Aunt Nettie said
lived up Inland Road near the Waterloos. Then there
were those of us somehow connected with the investigation into Hershel's death—Trey, Meg, Aunt Nettie,
me, and Chief Jones.

Trey, like the other men, wore Warner Pier dress-
up—khakis and a sports shirt—but Meg hadn't followed the "less black than the widow" rule. She had
on a sleeveless black linen dress and was wearing a
short strand of what I was sure were real pearls. There
were no chairs, and she kept shifting from foot to foot.
I guessed she was trying to keep her high heels from
sinking into the turf and thanked my lucky stars I'd
thought to wear flats.

Patsy was in navy blue and had regained her compo-
sure since the afternoon she'd almost accused Joe of
murdering her brother. The minister was mercifully
generic, relying on Bible verses and standard plati-
tudes. Which is sad in itself—I mean, when no one
can dredge up any happy memories of the deceased,
it's a sign of a wasted life.

Afterward, we shook hands and murmured at Patsy
and Frank and a cousin who had materialized from
Kalamazoo for the occasion. Then Aunt Nettie and I
started for her car. We were nearly there when I heard
rapid footsteps behind us. Trey called out, "Lee!"

I turned to see both Trey and Meg approaching Meg bore down on Aunt Nettie, neatly cutting her off, and Trey took me aside. "Were you serious about seeing Gray Gables?"

"I'd love to, Trey."

"It looks as if tonight would be a good time for a tour."

"Tonight?"

"I know that's pretty short notice. But my cousins are the actual owners, you know. They'll be coming this weekend and may stay the rest of the summer."

"Trey, I can see it another time. Next fall, next year."

"No, I have to be over there tonight anyway. I want to change the lock on the kitchen door. I'd be delighted to show you and Joe around." He leaned closer. "Please don't tell anyone. My cousins don't mind me showing people like you through, but they don't want—you know, public tours."

"Fine. As soon as I get back to the shop I'll call Joe and see if he can come."

"Just leave a message on my answering machine."

I told Trey nine-thirty was the earliest time I'd be able to take a tour, and I caught up with Meg and Aunt Nettie. Meg was talking hard about the Junior League of Grand Rapids, a topic which I knew did not interest Aunt Nettie in the slightest. Unless the group voted to buy chocolate.

Meg then began to ask me about the chase on the lake; apparently word was getting around town. Aunt Nettie and I extricated ourselves as quickly as possible. I again told Trey I'd call him, then we went back to the office. As soon as I was there, I went to the phone to call Joe to pass on Trey's invitation.

But Stacy headed me off. "Joe called," she said. She looked at a note she was holding. "He said he would be tied up all afternoon and evening. He said to tell you . . ." She referred to her note. "He said

Tell her not to do anything risky. Tell her to keep safe.' " She looked up. "What did he mean?"

I tried to smile. "I expect he wants me to stay home, to avoid highways and lakes," I said.

"Will you do what he says?"

I could tell my reputation as a feminist was on the line. "It seems to be a reasonable request," I said, considering the events of the past two evenings. Besides, I don't really have any particular place to go. I won't let his instructions keep me from anything I think is important."

We left it at that. I called Trey and left a message that Joe and I could not make a tour of Gray Gables that evening. I stayed in the office until nearly seven p.m.

Then I took my dinner break and went out and solved Hershel Perkins' murder.

CHOCOLATE CHAT

CHOCOLATE AND POLITICS

- Coffee, tea, and chocolate arrived in England at almost the same time, the mid-seventeenth century. Chocolate was advertised in a British newspaper as early as 1657.

- In Spain and France, chocolate had been a drink of the aristocracy, but in England it was offered to the public—along with coffee and tea—at a new institution, the coffeehouse.

- Coffee was the cheapest of the three new beverages. Chocolate cost a bit more, and tea was most expensive of all.

- The famous diarist Samuel Pepys (1633–1703) often recorded drinking chocolate, apparently at coffeehouses. This reflects the life of London at the time; coffeehouses were centers of discussion. Consequently they were also focal points for development of a new social institution—the political party. This made King Charles II uneasy, and in 1675 he ordered the coffeehouses closed. Public outcry kept the order from ever going into force.

- In line with the democratization of chocolate drinking, the English developed quicker, easier ways of preparing it. Most chocolate in seventeenth century Europe was prepared from powdered cakes. But it still had to be stirred all the time to keep it from separating. The French invented a special pot with a hole in the lid to make this easy.

Chapter 19

I didn't solve the murder on purpose. It was an acci
dental process that began when I stood up and
realized my pantyhose were drooping.

The sagging pantyhose were uncomfortable, of
course, and that discomfort made me aware that I
wasn't wearing one of my five pairs of comfy khaki
slacks, and being aware that I wasn't wearing one of
them reminded me that the newest pair had sunk in
Lake Michigan the previous evening. Then I remembered that Joe had mentioned walking up and down
the beach over by the old Root Beer Barrel to see if
the slacks had washed ashore.

Joe had apparently not been able to do that. But, I
decided, I could. Even though the chance of the slacks
washing ashore was remote.

Walking up and down the beach was not at all risky,
I assured myself. I could park at the Root Beer Barrel
site, cross Lake Shore Drive, climb down the bank,
and walk up and down the Lake Michigan beach as
far as I wanted to. Or as far as I had time to, because
I needed to get back to the shop and be there until
closing time.

So, shortly before seven o'clock, the time Tracy was

due back from her break, I phoned Mike's Sidewalk Café and ordered a sandwich to go. I put on the jacket I keep in the office. I found a pair of flip-flop rubber sandals in the van, then slipped out of my pumps and droopy pantyhose. I even grabbed a garbage bag big enough to hold the slacks. I was thinking positively. I might actually find them.

I picked up the sandwich—roast beef on rye with a side of slaw—and drove over to the former location of the Root Beer Barrel. This would be a private beach picnic. Quite a nice dinner break, whether I found the slacks or not.

There were no handy-dandy stairs leading down to the beach opposite the Root Beer Barrel property. But I located a path—fairly well-used—and slipped and slid thirty or forty feet down the sandy hill to the beach without getting my long black and white skirt too dirty or getting sand in my sandwich. I even found a big log that had drifted ashore and made a lovely spot to sit and eat my dinner. The wind had changed, and now the waves were coming from the northwest— just the opposite of the direction they'd been coming the night before. That was good; it meant that if the slacks washed up the beach, they might then have washed back down and stayed more or less even with the location where I'd lost them. Unless they'd sunk permanently in thirty feet of water.

I finished my sandwich, stuffed the trash in the sack the food had come in, tucked it into my big garbage bag, then walked down the beach. A walk on the beach is always a wonderful experience. The sun wasn't yet low enough to blind me if I looked out at the lake, and I strolled along, stepping over the stones and through the beach grass, shaking the sand out of my sandals now and then, keeping an eye on the time, and looking for those slacks.

I admit I was surprised when I found them.

By rights they should have been at the bottom of

e lake, but there they were—caught on a piece of
iftwood and wafting back and forth in the waves.
'hen I tried to pick them up, however, I nearly de-
ded to leave them there. They were heavy with
ater, and I wasn't dressed to wring them out. But I
restled them into the garbage bag and started lug-
ng the sack back up the beach.

I dreaded the climb back up the sand dunes. That's
hen it was going to be hard to keep my skirt clean.
guess that's why I eyed the stairways which led up
the cottages along the lake.

Not all lakeshore cottages have stairways down to
e beach. For people who can afford them, they're a
:ry nice amenity. But they're privately owned. The
:aches are public, but property owners have a right
get snotty if strangers walk up their stairs the way
e and I had the night before. The strangers wind
, as we had, in somebody's back yard. That's tres-
ssing. So I kept looking at the stairs, but I didn't
up any of them.

Then I recognized the stairs Joe and I had used the
ght before. They had a deck about halfway up that
as quite distinctive. A white-haired woman dressed
white shorts and a blue T-shirt was just coming
wn the stairs.

I stopped and called out to her. "Hello! Are you
e lady of the house?"

She nodded, narrowing her eyes slightly.

"I owe you an apology," I said. "We got a boat
ground last night, out on the sand bar, and we had
swim ashore. We used your stairs to get up to the
ad, and I'm afraid we trampled through your
wers."

"Oh!" The woman came a few steps down. "Thanks
r telling me. We thought we'd had window peepers."

"No, we didn't peep. We were mighty cold, so we
d knock at the door on your deck, but nobody
swered."

"What time was this?"

"Sometime after ten."

"We went to Holland to the late movie. I'm sorr we weren't here to answer the door. You must hav been frozen."

"I'm sorry about the flowers." By now the woma was nearly to the bottom of the stairs, so we intro duced ourselves. Her name was Carla Maples, and sh said she and her husband had moved to the cottag "full-time" after he retired.

She smiled broadly when I told her I was busines manager for TenHuis Chocolade. "I love that place Especially those almond-flavored truffles. Amaretto.'

" 'Milk chocolate interior coated in white choco late.' I like those, too. And now I need to get bac to work."

"Do you want to use the stairs again?"

"That would be a big help. I'm parked down by th old Root Beer Barrel property, and there aren't an stairs down there."

"It's a couple of blocks away, but we can see tha area from our front yard," Mrs. Maples said. She le me up the stairs. I admired her flowers and her hous and didn't say too much about why Joe and I ha been swimming ashore, instead of waiting for someon to get us off the sandbar.

We skirted the house on stepping stones Joe and had missed in the moonlight, then came out on Lak Shore Drive. Mrs. Maples gestured in the direction c the Root Beer Barrel in a genteel manner. "We use to be able to see the old Barrel through the trees i the winter. I was really surprised when it blew down.

A faint hope stirred. "You didn't see it happer did you?"

"No. We were in Florida for the month of March and it was gone when we got back. I've heard a rumo that the property may be redeveloped."

I decided I didn't have time to go into all the de

ils. "I've heard that, too. I'm sure that all the neigh-
ors around here would like to see something built
here. The site is an eyesore as it is."

Mrs. Maples sighed. "It's not just that particular lot.
's that whole stretch. The old motel—that's almost
vergrown now. And the DeBoer House. That's a
eautiful structure, but you can't even see it now. It's
oo bad that something can't be done with it."

We shook hands and I made a mental note to write
Irs. Maples a thank-you note and to give her some
hocolates. Then I walked on up the Lake Shore Drive
oward my car. The episode didn't amount to much,
ut it was significant because it caused me to approach
e Root Beer Barrel site from a different direction.
d never come toward it from the south before.

I decided Stacy and Tracy could manage without
e for another five minutes. I wanted to get a look
this DeBoer house everybody kept raving about.

It took me the whole five minutes to figure out how
approach it. There was a heavy bank of trees and
rubs between it and Joe's property, but I finally
und a pathway from the main road, beat my way
rough—I should have been wearing jungle gear, not
ankle-length skirt and flip-flops—and came out of
e bushes around thirty feet from a beautiful, broad
eranda.

I stood there looking at that veranda, the graceful
eps leading up to it, the picturesque turrets at the
orners of the building. Then I swung back and
eeked through the bushes in the direction of the Old
nglish Motel. I couldn't see it because of the heavy
ndergrowth. But I knew it was there.

And I also knew who had killed Hershel, and I
new why.

"Oh, my stars!" I said. I turned and made wh
eed I could getting down that overgrown path b
the road. Then I tried to run for the van—not
asiest thing to do wearing flip-flops. I stumble

slid, but I finally made it, dug my keys from m
pocket, jumped in the van, and sped toward town.

My mind was racing madly. I had to tell Chie
Jones. I had to tell Joe. I had to tell somebody.

I parked in the alley behind TenHuis Chocolade
unlocked the back door, and dashed in. Tracy an
Stacy stared at me openmouthed as I rushed by them
without speaking and snatched up the telephone. I hi
the speed dial for Joe's number, then hung up. Hi
phone was tapped, and he'd told me the chief wante
to leave it that way. I punched in his cell phone num
ber. It rang and rang, then I got some electronic mes
sage box in some office someplace far away. I hun
up on the electronic voice.

Chief Jones. That was the person I really needed
City Hall was closed, of course. I thumbed throug
the telephone book until I found his home numbe
But when I dialed it, he didn't answer either.

I did, however, leave a message on his answerin
machine. And it wasn't just "call me." I left the nam
of Hershel's murderer.

I wasn't through. I called the city hall number, usin
the trick Joe had used the night when we found Her
shel's body. The answering machine picked up, and
yelled for the dispatcher. But nobody came to th
phone.

Finally, I called 9-1-1 and identified myself. "It'
imperative that I reach Chief Hogan Jones," I said.

"The Warner Pier police chief?"

"Yes."

"This is the Warner County Sheriff's office. Th
Warner Pier Police Station is not available. I can har
dle any emergency."

"No. I need Chief Jones."

"Chief Jones is not on duty."

"But this is about the murder of Hershel Perkins
I must talk to him immediately."

"I don't believe he's available."

"I know you can page him. This is an emergency! Please."

"I'll try to reach him, but what sort of emergency do you have?"

I didn't answer. It was going to be terribly hard to explain.

She kept talking. "Fire? Accident? Crime? I need to know who to send."

I thought another minute, then spoke. "It's not that kind of an emergency. I'm sorry I bothered you."

I hung up. After all, what was my hurry? It wasn't as if the killer was likely to flee to Canada that night. I'd keep trying to reach Chief Jones, but the killer would still be in Warner Pier the next morning. After all, Hershel had been killed partly to protect the killer's place in the community—or so I thought. The killer wasn't going to throw it up now, not unless the killer learned that I'd tumbled to what happened.

At least, I'd believe that was the truth if I could find Joe. Where was he? Joe didn't know who the murderer was, and I believed he was meant to be a second victim. If nothing else, the killer's attempts to chase us down with a panel truck and with a stolen boat proved that.

Joe could be in deadly danger, and I didn't know how to warn him.

I halfheartedly tried to call Jerry Cherry, but I wasn't even surprised that he didn't answer his phone. Then I looked out at the shop. At least a dozen customers were standing in line. Tracy and Stacy needed a couple of extra hands. I didn't know what else to do, so I went out to help them.

As I served out Frangelico truffles ("Hazelnut interior with milk chocolate coating, sprinkled with nougat") and cute little chocolate lizards, I tried to remember what Joe had said when he had talked to

Stacy. And he'd said nothing. Just that he was going to be tied up that evening. But why had he turned off his cell phone? Where was he?

As the rush began to clear, I looked across the street at Joe's mom's office. There was a light. So, as soon as the front counter was down to two groups of customers, I went into the office and called her. Maybe Joe had told her where he was going.

But she said he hadn't. "I haven't talked to him since this morning, Lee. He called and told me not to use his landline. Do you know what all that was about?"

"It's a long story." I hesitated. "Mercy, I think I've figured out who killed Hershel Perkins. And I think Joe is next on the list. I've tried every way I know to reach Chief Jones, and I can't find him either. I've simply got to find Joe and warn him. Do you have any ideas?"

I'd been counting on Mercy not to panic, and she didn't. "Actually, he could be out at the shop. If he turned the cell phone off . . . Or he might have left a note on his calendar. Something simple like that."

Or he could be lying out there in a pool of blood. Mercy's idea made sense. "I'll go see if he's there," I said.

"We'll both go. I'll pick you up." Mercy hung up.

I once again ran off and left Tracy and Stacy with the shop. By now it was nearly nine, close to closing time. I didn't give them any explanation, and they both looked amazed, but I grabbed my purse and ran out the front door, still wearing my flip-flops, long skirt, and jacket.

Mercy and I didn't talk as we drove out to Joe's shop. About halfway there I suddenly fantasized that he might have another woman out there. That would certainly be an explanation of why he was "tied up all evening." And it might explain why he'd turned off the cell phone.

I could be headed toward an end to our relationship. But I was so worried about his safety that I didn't care.

It was not yet dark. In June in southwest Michigan the sun doesn't set until after nine-thirty, another situation that amazes the Texan in me. Somehow it doesn't seem decent for the sun to stay up that late.

I felt a wave of relief when we pulled into Joe's parking area, and I saw his pickup in its usual spot. But all the doors to the shop were closed, and the place looked deserted. The sedan was not tied up at the dock. Mercy and I got out and pounded on the door. Nobody answered our summons.

We spoke to each other almost in unison. "Do you have a key?"

Then we both sighed and did our unison act again. "No."

"I'll get the one from behind the downspout," I said.

The key container was very low down and flat against the steel building. I waved the box at Mercy, then came back to the door. The key worked immediately.

It might not have been dark outside, but inside the shop was like the old Smothers Brothers song which describes falling into a vat of chocolate. Dark chocolate. The only windows are in the office and in Joe's one-room apartment, and the doors to both places were closed.

I felt for the switch beside the door. As the banks of fluorescent lights flashed on, I called out, "Joe!"

My voice reverberated around the big steel building. I went first to the office, then to Joe's apartment, opening the doors and calling out. No answer. Both rooms were empty.

When I came out of the apartment, Mercy was in the office. She pointed to the desk. "What's this about?"

On the desk was a tape recorder. It was sitting next to the telephone. A long cord went from it to a round rubber deal that was attached to the side of the phone.

I'd seen a similar setup. "It's a microphone," I said. "At one of the office jobs I had I used one of those to record reports the salesmen called in."

"A bug?"

"You could use it that way. But it's usually used to record your own calls."

Mercy reached for the tape recorder and flipped the lid open. A tape was inside. "Maybe this will tell us something," she said.

She rewound the tape, then hit the "play" button.

"Hello." Joe's voice began.

"Listen, Joe, we need to talk. You've figured out that I'm involved in this Root Beer Barrel deal, haven't you?"

"I was beginning to get that idea."

"I suppose you found my link to Tom Johnson."

"It wasn't too hard."

"I can explain all that. But I don't want to do it on the telephone. Can you meet me at Gray Gables?"

"Why there?"

"Because it will be completely private. I'm in Grand Rapids, and I won't be back until around nine. I've got to go over there this evening. We'll be able to hash the whole thing out."

"Around nine?"

"I'll leave the gate unlocked for you."

"Don't bother. I'll come in the boat."

The call ended. Mercy and I were staring at each other wide-eyed.

She spoke first. "That was Trey's voice!"

"My God!" I said. "Joe's agreed to meet the murderer all alone and on his own turf! We've got to stop him."

Chapter 20

Neither Mercy nor I is the type to stand around
wringing our hands. She headed for the door, and
beat her to it. The only reason I was there first was
because Mercy had whipped a cell phone out of her
purse and was talking as we ran.

"Mike! Mike! Emergency!" she was saying.

She was jamming the cell phone back in the purse
as we got to the door. Luckily that door had an auto-
matic lock. We ran for her car so fast that we would
have left it standing open.

"Mike can track down Chief Jones if anybody can,"
she said. "But he didn't pick up his cell phone. Let's
head for city hall. You drive. I'll keep phoning."

"There's nobody at city hall tonight, is there? I
called and got the county operator."

"The local dispatcher must have been on her dinner break."

Mercy handed me her keys, and I got behind the
wheel of her car. I burned rubber getting out of there.
Mercy—proving herself a real insurance woman—dug
a phone book out of the back seat and began calling
Mike Herrera's restaurants. He wasn't at Herrera's.
He wasn't at Mike's Sidewalk Café. He wasn't at the

Waterside. By the time she'd screamed "Emergency!" and her cell phone number at someone at each restaurant, we were at city hall. I skidded into a parking spot normally reserved for one of the Warner Pier patrol cars, and we both jumped out. Mercy ran to the side door and began to pound on it. I could see the dispatcher jumping to her feet inside.

"You tell her what's happened," I said. "I'm going to try something else."

I turned and ran down the street, flipping and flopping in those darn rubber beach sandals toward the alley behind TenHuis Chocolade. If Trey was at Gray Gables, I believed that I would be able to get inside.

I rushed to my van, flipped the rear door up, and scrabbled through the stuff I'd tossed in over the weeks and months. I might be determined to face down a murderer, but I didn't want to do it without a weapon of some sort. But I couldn't think of anything lethal in my van.

To my surprise, over in one corner I found a lucky stone, one of the ones I'd found in May when Joe and I picnicked. The average lucky stone, I'd guess, weighs three ounces; they're usually pretty small. But this was one of the atypical ones—a three-pound number, even bigger than the one we'd left beside Joe's shop, the one Trey had used to kill Hershel. And I found a chamois my father had given me for washing the van.

I wrapped the lucky stone in the chamois and put the improvised weapon in my purse. It seemed to be poetic justice. I was quite prepared to kill Trey Corbett with the same sort of weapon he'd used on Hershel.

I had just started the van when Aunt Nettie appeared in the back door of the shop.

"Lee!"

I punched the button that lowered the passenger-side window. "I can't talk! Got to go! Joe's in trouble!"

I backed out and drove away wondering why she'd come back to the shop. There was no way she could know about Joe being in danger. I could have used help, true, but I didn't want to involve Aunt Nettie. She's not frail; she's stronger and healthier than I am. But despite the rock, I didn't intend to use violence on Trey. I intended to use guile to distract him, to keep him from harming Joe until Mercy could get the police there. I didn't see how Aunt Nettie could fit into this plan.

I would simply go to the gate of the estate, then honk my horn to attract attention. I'd claim that I had found out that Joe was, after all, able to make the tour of Gray Gables, so I'd decided to join the two of them.

The big risk was that Trey would kill Joe as soon as he got there. I pushed that possibility into my subconscious.

My plan, like most of the ones I make, fell apart almost immediately. When I got to Gray Gables, the gate was locked, as I'd expected. But when I honked, nothing happened.

I could see that same corner of the house through the trees. But I sat there honking while the hands of my watch whirled through six minutes, and no one came to the gate. No Trey came walking or driving up the drive to the gate. Nothing. Gray Gables, for all intents, was deserted.

Well, if I couldn't get in through the gate, I'd have to do it another way. I backed up, then turned, backed, and turned. After doing this several times, I managed to get the van sideways in the drive, almost touching the gate. I'd climb on the top of the van and get over that way.

But when I opened the door and got out of the van—I'd decided to use the back seat as a ladder—a voice boomed out of bushes.

"Ms. McKinney! What in the world are you doing?"

I nearly fell flat on my flitter. Then I realized it was Dolly Jolly—all six feet three or four inches and 250 pounds of her. Well, of course. She'd heard me honking, even if Trey hadn't.

And I also realized she might tell me how to get into Gray Gables without risking my neck by tumbling over that wrought-iron gate. Dolly Jolly lived in a cottage that was almost on the grounds of Gray Gables. I couldn't believe she wouldn't have peeked inside the property. Maybe she would help me.

"Dolly! I've got to get into Gray Gables. Can you show me a back way?"

She frowned. "I think they keep the gate locked because they want to keep people out!"

"It's a matter of life and death!"

She lowered her voice to a dull roar that she probably intended as a whisper. "There's something going on over there tonight. Better stay away."

"No! That's what I'm afraid of. Oh, God, it's too long a story, but my boyfriend's been lured over there by a killer! The police are on the way, but Joe doesn't know he's in danger and I've got to warn him!"

I realized I had closed in on Dolly and I was gripping her arm. I tried to back off. "Please. It's really important."

Dolly sighed. "Well, if you've called the police . . . I guess I could go over there with you. Keep an eye on things."

"Anything! But I've got to get in."

"There's a better way than climbing over the gate." She led me through the bushes, down the path that she'd used to confront Lindy and me. The sun was nearly down to the horizon—miles away over Lake Michigan—and the woods were growing dark. I glimpsed a simple little house, but Dolly walked past it, following a path that led back toward the left. "There's a gap in the fence," she said. She was still trying to talk quietly. "Probably something to do with the hobo jungle!"

We got through a line of shrubs and came to a high, chain-link fence. Then we turned right and followed the fence. I don't know how far we went, but she suddenly grasped the woven wire and pulled it back. We'd come to the gap. I went through the fence, then pushed at the wire to keep the gap open for Dolly. Inside the fence was more undergrowth, but there was definitely a path. And after twenty or twenty-five steps, we came to a cleared area with large trees here and there. The giant house—three stories of turrets, gables, and porches—loomed between us and the river. The last rays of the sun were slicing through the trees, but the half-mile of woods between the mansion and the lake meant that we were in heavy shade. Inside the house, it would have been dark. And there were no lights in any of the windows.

I whispered. "They've simply got to be there."

"Let's go around the house," Dolly said. She really was speaking quietly now.

We turned left and circled the house. There was a sidewalk, but we stayed away from it, keeping our distance from the structure. When we rounded the end, we saw the broad lawn leading down to the river. But that side of the house was dark, too, and no doors were open. The whole area was quiet. We could hear a motorboat down on the river, but nothing any closer made a sound.

Had I been wrong? Was Joe not there? Or had Trey already attacked him? Killed him? Dumped him in the river? I shivered all over. Then I pointed. "There's a car!"

It was Trey's SUV. It was parked about a hundred yards away, close to a long wooden shed. The shed, I realized in a minute, was down by the river.

"It's by the boathouse," Dolly said.

"Of course! Joe came in his boat."

To my relief I saw that the structure she described as the boathouse had no windows on the side facing us. I began to run toward it, realizing that people inside would not be able to see me approaching unless they came outside. Dolly Jolly followed me, also running. Two big, tall women jogging down the lawn.

When we got near the boathouse, I slowed down and tiptoed. After a few more steps I could hear voices. Just a murmur, but two men were talking. I moved closer, planting my feet firmly, daring those darn sandals to make a flip or a flop.

The boathouse was an old wooden building, more of a work shed for storing boats in the winter than a place for them to be tied up. I couldn't see that any boats were around. Probably the building was open on the other side, with a dock going out into the water.

I was concentrating so hard on being quiet that a sudden thud made me jump and whirl around. It was a car door slamming, up near the road.

Dolly had turned toward it, too. I leaned close to her. "Maybe it's the cops," I said. "Can you go back and let them in?" She hesitated. "Please."

She nodded and started back up the lawn, walking fast, but obviously trying to keep quiet.

I went around the corner of the boathouse, looking for an entrance. I found a door, and I touched the handle. It moved. I was able to crack the door—just slightly. I got ready to do my act: Throw the door open and walk in demanding a tour.

Then I heard Joe's voice.

"I think I've earned a cut," he said. "I don't know why everybody in Warner Pier thinks I'm not interested in money. I am."

"You could have made a lot more practicing law than you're likely to repairing boats." It was Trey's voice.

"Yeah, and be stuck in an office in a suit my whole
life. Having to kowtow to the client. You don't like
that. Why should I? But I don't object to making
money. I like to think I'm not greedy, but I don't see
why I shouldn't get in on this sweet deal you've come
up with."

A cut? A deal? What was Joe talking about? I
necked through the crack, but I couldn't see anything
but a bunch of junk. I saw weathered oars, rusty fishing tackle boxes, a couple of antique wooden barrels,
scrap wood, tangled wire—just general trash. But
there was no sign of either Joe or Trey.

I looked around the outside of the building, and I
spotted a window. It was about six feet farther down
the wall and rather high. But it wasn't too high for a
tall woman to look through. I stood on tiptoe and
looked inside. Now I could see that the shed really
was a boathouse. The opposite end was open to the
river, and I could even see Joe's sedan tied up just
outside. I could see Joe and Trey, too. They were
standing inside the door I'd been peeking through. If
I had looked in the door, they definitely would have
seen me.

Joe spoke again. "Anyway, Trey, I ought to thank
you for pulling the Root Beer Barrel down. It needed
to be done, and I wouldn't have known how to do it."

"That was easy. I just put a rope around it, borrowed a big truck, and pulled."

"How did Hershel get involved?"

Trey laughed. It wasn't a pleasant sound. "Stupid
jerk! He was always prowling around."

"I guess you told him I did it."

"I didn't have to. He came to me, told me about
seeing the truck over there, then seeing the Barrel go
down. It mystified the poor jerk. All I had to do was
point out that it was going to be a lot easier for the
property owner to redevelop that lot if an Act of God
got rid of the Barrel."

"But you didn't like it when he accused me—to my face—of pulling it down."

"As long as you thought it blew down—well, you were doing exactly what I needed done. If you got too curious, I didn't know what would happen."

Joe's voice became cold. "I ought to punch you until your teeth rattle, Trey. There was no need to try to kill me. And Lee!"

"Oh, those weren't serious attempts, Joe." Like heck, I thought, remembering that cold swim and that scary ride in Joe's pickup. "I just wanted to distract you."

"Well, I didn't appreciate it—whatever you had in mind. So I don't expect us to become close friends over this, Trey. But there's no reason we can't be business partners. What are you planning to do with that strip, anyway?"

"What do you mean?"

"Today I talked to the people who own the DeBoer House and the Old English Motel. Tom Johnson is dealing with them, too. That's nearly a city block long. You've obviously got bigger plans than some little restaurant or motel on the site of the Root Beer Barrel."

It took all my self-control to keep from going to the door, throwing it open, striding inside, and telling Joe just what Trey's plan was. But I didn't understand the conversation I was hearing. Joe was trying to cut himself in on the deal? He didn't mind making money? That was probably true, but he certainly hadn't talked to me like that. I didn't want to believe that Joe would go along with anything crooked, and what Trey had done—pulling down the Root Beer Barrel—was illegal. Killing Hershel was even more illegal. But now Joe was proposing to participate in whatever Trey was up to. I was more confused with each word I heard from Joe.

But it was Trey's next words that really caught me by surprise.

"We can go into the details later. And we might be
ble to work out some kind of a deal, but if we do,
here's one perk you're not going to get. From now
n, you're going to stay away from my wife."

Chapter 21

I gasped, but luckily Joe gasped even louder, hiding the noise I'd made. Then he laughed.

"Maggie Mae—I mean, Meg—is a very pretty woman. But if you think we're fooling around, you've got it all wrong."

"You dated her."

"When I was seventeen! She was sixteen. It's ancient history. I hadn't seen her again until you two moved back to Warner Pier. Then maybe we'd see each other in the checkout line at the Superette. I've never even been alone with her since we got out of high school. Fifteen years!"

"She said she slept with you."

Joe was silent a minute. "I don't know why she'd tell you that."

"Because I asked her!" Trey yelled it out.

Joe yelled his answer. "Then you're dumber than you have a right to be!"

I expected that Trey would yell back and that the argument would escalate. It didn't worry me too much; I was sure that if it came to a fight Joe could turn Trey inside out.

But that's not what happened. Instead, Trey gulped

ree times. I could see his Adam's apple move up
nd down as he swallowed his anger. Then the one eye
I could see narrowed craftily and he spoke. "Maybe I
verreacted. Maybe she was teasing me."

"That's got to be the answer, Trey. There's nothing
etween Meg and me."

Trey nodded. "But you asked about what I planned
or the Lake Shore Drive site. Let me show you."

Had he brought the drawing here? To the boat-
ouse? I watched as Trey turned and gestured toward
large table behind him. The table was covered with
sheet, which he carefully removed, folding it and
ying it aside.

And there, displayed under the bare bulbs of the
oathouse, was a four-foot-long model of the structure
d seen in the drawing—the beautiful Victorian re-
ort hotel.

It incorporated the Old English Motel in the form
f a mock Victorian village, and it used the DeBoer
louse as the main hotel. But there were no remains
f the old Root Beer Barrel in between. On the model
ie motel and the historic home were linked by pictur-
sque cottages. A swimming pool and elaborate land-
caping completed the model.

The old Root Beer Barrel would definitely not have
t in.

Joe whistled. "Wow! What a layout." He leaned
ver, concentrating on the model.

Trey leaned over, too, and to Joe it probably
eemed that he was also admiring his model. But I
ould see his right hand. I could see it move behind
ie table's leg and bring out a metal bar. I caught a
limpse of the split end, and I recognized it. It was a
mall crowbar.

Trey did not need a small crowbar to show Joe a
1odel of a resort hotel. He definitely had another plan
or the tool. I reached into my purse and grasped my
wn weapon, the lucky stone wrapped in a chamois.

Trey straightened up, but I didn't wait for him to hit Joe with the crowbar. I yanked out my improvised sling—sending my purse flying—and I smashed the window I was looking through.

Then I began to yell, and I ran for the door, hoping the smash and noise would distract Trey from his attack on Joe.

I plunged through the door and into the harsh light of the boathouse.

Trey was gawking over his shoulder, looking toward the window, but Joe had already taken action. He was reaching for Trey's hand, the hand that held the crowbar.

Then—well, all hell broke loose.

A tarp in the back seat of Joe's sedan lurched as if a small earthquake had hit it. It was thrown back and Jerry Cherry popped up. The boat rocked wildly as he scrambled onto the dock.

Footsteps pounded outside the boathouse, the door I'd come in was smashed back against the wall, and a whole crowd ran in. I was so confused I could barely identify them as Mercy Woodyard, Mike Herrera, Dolly Jolly, and Aunt Nettie.

Then a loudspeaker started booming. "This is the police! Put down your weapons! Come out with your hands raised!"

The boathouse wasn't really big enough for all this activity. Especially since Joe and Trey were now having a wrestling match under the table that held the model. I danced around, trying to get a chance use my lucky-stone sling—rather hard to do when your intended target is under a table.

Mercy was yelling, and she and Mike fell to their knees. Each of them grabbed for one of Trey's flailing feet. But the feet were flailing too hard; they couldn't catch hold of them.

Then Joe rolled on top of Trey, and the two of them hit the table leg. The table jumped and the

model went flying. Trey screamed like a wounded she-
bear. They rolled again, this time out from under the
table. I began to swing my weapon, something like
little David getting ready for Goliath, but I was afraid
I'd hit Joe. So I just kept swinging it around.

Joe and Trey flipped one more time, and this time
they were close to the water. I thought both of them
were going to go in, right between the dock and the
sedan.

And finally—finally—Jerry Cherry was able to get
through the crowd and grab Trey. He and Joe wrestled
Trey face down onto the dock. He couldn't move,
though his feet were still flailing.

Dolly poked her head over my shoulder. "Do you
want me to sit on him?" she said.

"Nah," the voice came from the darkness. "I think
we can manage now."

Chief Hogan Jones and the other two members of
the Warner Pier Police Force came in through a door
near the open end of the boathouse.

Then all of us—Joe, Jerry, Chief Jones, Mercy,
Mike, Dolly, Aunt Nettie, and me—said the same
thing, in unison.

"What are you doing here?"

By the time Chief Jones and Jerry Cherry had Trey
handcuffed, and Chief Jones had sent one of the patrol
officers for a car to come and get him, we'd begun to
sort it out. Apparently three separate groups had decided Joe needed rescuing and had taken on the job.

Aunt Nettie was the one who mystified me. "How
did you get involved?" I asked her. "What were you
doing at the shop? I thought you were safely home
in bed."

"Stacy called me," she said. "She said you had gone
tearing out of there with Mercy. She and Tracy overheard you leaving a message for Chief Jones. She
thought I'd like to know."

"I don't know if I should be mad at her or at you."

"All's well, Lee. Joe's okay, and I guess Hogan go the goods on Trey Corbett."

Joe joined the conversation then. "That's what I'n afraid isn't true," he said. He unbuttoned his shirt an pulled something electronic out.

I stared, then realized what it must be. "You wer wired!"

"Yeah, yeah. It's certainly reassuring to know tha my nearest and dearest friends and relatives—my girl friend, my mom—all thought I was dumb enough t have a one-on-one meeting in a secluded spot wit a murderer."

"That's why you kept asking Trey to cut you in o the deal!"

"You heard that? Chief Jones and I were trying t get him to admit he killed Hershel."

"So the whole thing is on tape."

"Not that it's going to do much good." Joe looke at the chief.

Hogan Jones frowned. "We can get him for the at tacks on you and Lee."

"But doesn't that prove he killed Hershel?" I said

The chief and Joe shook their heads in unison "Nope," Joe said. "If I were still a defense attorney I'd have a great time with that recording. All it doe is establish me as a crook."

"And now," Chief Jones said. "I'd appreciate a of you stepping outside. I have permission from Jin Corbett, the owner of this property, to search. Tre was apparently using this building for the projects h wanted to keep quiet, and there's always the possibil ity we will find some evidence that Hershel was here Not that it will do much good."

Mercy spoke that time. "Why not? If you can prov Hershel was here . . ."

"It won't prove a thing," Joe said. "He probably had been here. It's established that Hershel followe Trey around. Even if the chief finds Hershel's finger

rints on every inch of this boathouse, it won't prove
e was here the night he was killed."

I was feeling extremely dispirited as I turned to fol-
ow the group outside. We picked our way through all
he junk carefully, but it was too late. We'd had good
ntentions, but we'd definitely contaminated the
rime scene.

It was Mike Herrera who stumbled and kicked the
rash basket over. Sawdust, hunks of plastic, paint
ans, scrap wood—everything dumped out in a heap
n the floor.

Mike growled and leaned down as if he were going
o scoop it all back up.

"Leave it!" The chief's voice was sharp. "We'd have
o go through that basket anyway."

But Aunt Nettie had already leaned over. "Oh,
ook," she said. "A TenHuis box."

And there, covered with sawdust, was a white box
ied with a blue ribbon. I didn't need to see the snazzy
ans serif type in the corner to recognize it. It was the
ind of a box we use for a pound of chocolates. Or
or a fancy molded chocolate item.

"Chief!" I almost jumped up and down. "If there's
a bog in that fox it will prove Hershel was here the
ight he disappeared! I mean, a frog! In the box!"

"Oh, yes!" Aunt Nettie said. She looked nearly as
xcited as I did. "Hershel bought one of our eight-
unce white chocolate frogs the afternoon he disap-
eared. I packed it for him personally—in a box just
ike that one. It's the only one we've sold so far. If
hat's the frog . . ."

Chief Jones knelt and looked at the box. "Let's get
ome photos before we look inside," he said.

He motioned all of us non-lawmen on out the door.
We stood around, talking excitedly. Through the door
we'd come out, we could see flashbulbs now and then.
But it was nearly ten minutes before the chief came
ut, carrying a brown paper sack.

"I guess I'll never get all of you to go home unless you see what was in the box," he said. He spread the top of the sack open, and held it out at arm's length. "Nettie, we'll let you peek first."

I knew what it was as soon as I saw her face, but my heart was pounding as I took the second peek.

Nestled inside the box, wrapped in tissue paper, was a big white chocolate frog with dark chocolate spots on his back.

"Yee-haw!" I said.

It's hard to do a group hug when you're jumping up and down, but we managed.

Chapter 22

There's one nice thing about hanging out with foodies. First, Aunt Nettie insisted that everybody come by TenHuis Chocolade for a talk session and some chocolate, and Mike immediately said he'd bring coffee. Nobody said no. Aunt Nettie, Mercy, Mike, Dolly Jolly, Joe, and I all met in our break room. Mike brought two party-sized Thermoses of coffee and a bottle of brandy. Nobody said no to that, either.

After Aunt Nettie had served up a plate of truffles, bonbons, and solid chocolate—but no chocolate frogs—Joe wanted to know how I figured out Trey was the bad guy, and I wanted to know how he and Chief Jones figured it out.

Joe took an Italian cherry bonbon ("Amareena cherry in syrup and white chocolate cream") and started talking. "You remember I was going to ask a few questions about Tom Johnson? I turned my pal Webb Bartlett loose on the project."

Webb Bartlett is a law school buddy of Joe's who practices in Grand Rapids. He's one of those people who knows practically everybody in the world and if he doesn't know them, he know somebody else who does.

"Webb discovered Tom had been involved with a crooked developer who had conned a Grand Rapids architect. Webb knew the architect, so he called him and found out Trey used to work for his firm. And yes, Trey had been around when the architect got involved with Tom Johnson. So Trey had known Tom. That established a link. The chief had thought all along that Trey's story about being sideswiped by that black panel truck sounded fishy. Besides, another witness you and I didn't know about . . ."—Was it my imagination, or did Dolly Jolly's natural ruddiness grow even redder?—"had seen something that involved Trey. So I was able to convince Chief Jones that Tom Johnson was probably fronting for Trey, who must be the actual buyer for the old Root Beer Barrel property."

"But why couldn't Trey simply buy the property in the regular way?"

"Because he sat on the Historic District Commission."

"That doesn't mean he can't own and develop property in Warner Pier."

"No, but it does mean he's not supposed to vote on issues he's personally involved in. And he wanted to vote on demolishing the old Root Beer Barrel. So he had to make it appear that he had the idea for the resort and bought the property after—*after*—the Barrel had been torn down. Plus, Trey must have had money problems. I've gathered that he's a sort of poor relation to the wealthy side of the Corbett family. Buying a whole block of lakefront property would take a bundle of money. Maybe two bundles. He didn't have it."

"He'd have to have major financing to get that much money together," I said. "He couldn't do it without bringing in partners."

"I don't think Trey wanted partners. From what Webb picked up from Trey's former boss, he fired Trey because Trey's not a team player. He's the kind of architect who wants to make all the decisions on a project. He didn't want to build buildings that suited the client—the kind that architects actually get paid for."

"That fits with what Frank Waterloo said about him," I said. "Trey made all the decisions on their renovation—just let Patsy make the 'final choice' on the wallpaper." Since I had the floor, I described finding the elevation showing Trey's plan for the site and how I had later recognized the site after I got a look at the DeBoer House.

"Meg nearly had a fit when she realized I'd seen the drawing," I said. "At the time I didn't understand why. I'm guessing that Trey figured out the justification—I mean, juxtaposition!—the relationship of the Old English Motel and the DeBoer House, and he saw the potential for the site to become a re-creation of a turn of the twentieth century resort. But the Root Beer Barrel was 1940s commercial. It didn't fit in with his ideas."

"He'd been urging me to petition the commission for permission to take the Barrel down," Joe said. "If I had, then my guess is he would have backed the idea and voted for it. Then he would have 'discovered' the site's potential and bought it. But he was probably afraid someone was going to beat him to the property. Maybe the high winds in that last winter storm gave him the idea. I think he simply saw a chance to take a shortcut, get rid of the Barrel faster than he could legally. So he must have borrowed a heavy truck from some of his builder pals, then gone over there and pulled the old Barrel down.

"Unfortunately, Hershel saw what happened. He probably didn't see who was in the truck, but he mentioned it to Trey. Trey let him think I had done it.

But I knew I hadn't. If Hershel had accused me to my face—an event that became more and more likely as Hershel kept sulking about the situation—I was going to deny it. Then I might actually quiz Hershel, might figure out someone really had pulled the Barrel down. If it got out that Trey, a member of the Historic District Commission, had illegally torn a building down—well, the fine wouldn't be much, but it would pretty well finish his business in Warner Pier."

"So Trey decided to kill Hershel," I said.

"Right." Joe reached for a Bailey's Irish Cream bonbon ("Classic cream liqueur interior"). "And let's get one thing straight. We're talking murder in the first degree here. This was no crime of impulse. Trey had to set up his own alibis. Remember how he kept telling everybody he'd been working on the fireplace at the Miller cottage, even if we didn't ask where he'd been? He had to call me, pretend to be a potential boat buyer, and send me on a wild goose chase up to Saugatuck. He had to cut my phone line, so that nobody could just happen to call me at a moment that would have been inconvenient for him. Sometime in there he stole that lucky stone he used to kill Hershel from outside the shop. I can't swear he took the shop rag from my box of rags, because they're too common. But that would have been easy to do."

"One thing really puzzles me," I said. "Did Trey first cut your phone line, then tap it? Frankly, that doesn't make a lot of sense."

"It puzzles me, too. I wonder if he didn't do it the other way around—maybe it's been tapped for a long time."

"Why?" Mercy asked.

"Apparently Trey had gotten the idea that Meg was seeing another man. I suspect that he was checking to see if she and I had revived our teenaged affair." Joe took my hand. "I'm happy to say, first, we hadn't and second, neither Lee nor I like to talk dirty on the phone."

We all laughed, but the idea of Trey listening in on our calls was—well, nasty. I took the taste out of my mouth with a sip of brandy and a mocha pyramid.

"I wonder if he didn't even goad Hershel into attacking you at the post office," I said. "If he was already determined to frame you . . . You wouldn't have been such a ready-made suspect if it weren't for that little set-to."

"Unless Trey tells us, we'll never know the answer to that one," Joe said.

I went on. "But whose boat did he use to run the *Toadfrog* down? His boat, the *Nutmeg,* is too small. Plus, it would have left evidence."

Joe shook his head. "I always thought running down Hershel's canoe was an awfully iffy way to kill him, and I don't believe it happened that way."

"What do you think happened?"

"I've suggested to Chief Jones that the state police crime lab people look around outside at Gray Gables. If I were going to make a canoe look as if it had been hit by a bigger boat, I'd simply put it up against some sort of pole—on a tennis court, maybe, or a flagpole—tie a rope around it lengthwise and attach the rope to my pickup. Then I'd pull. Those aluminum canoes are not exactly battleships."

"That's almost exactly what he did!" We all jumped as Dolly Jolly's voice boomed out.

"Oh!" I said. "The chief told me that you saw more than you realized. Was that what you saw?"

"Didn't see him bending the canoe! Saw him dragging it up onto the lawn!" She turned to Joe. "He painted a board red and nailed it to a tree!"

"Sure! He needed paint that would match the runabout. That makes perfect sense."

Dolly Jolly cleared her throat. She helped herself

to an amaretto truffle ("Milk chocolate interior flavored with almond liqueur"). "Don't want all of you to think I'm just a snoop! The owners of Gray Gables—cousins of this Trey Corbett—they asked me to look around, keep an eye on the property! Think they realized he'd been using the boathouse for some private project. One reason they rented me the old cottage!"

We all nodded wisely. It seemed logical that Trey's relatives would have been suspicious.

"Meanwhile," I said, "I guess Trey lured Hershel to Gray Gables, hit him in the head, and left him unconscious. He must have planned to throw him in the water and leave him to drown."

"Yeah," Joe said. "He'd already sent me off to Saugatuck so I wouldn't have an alibi. But Hershel must have come to and staggered off. As I understand head injuries, Hershel may not have remembered what happened to him, but he probably knew it was something bad. But this was Hershel, who wasn't always logical even when he hadn't been hit in the head. Instead of calling an ambulance or the cops or going to Ms. Jolly's house for help, he got across the river somehow. Maybe just walked across on the Haven Road bridge. He was probably headed for the old chapel."

"Which," I said, "Patsy said he regarded as a refuge."

"Right," Joe said. "He hid in the woods around the chapel, then tried to get hold of Nettie, because he trusted her."

Aunt Nettie shook her head sadly. "But Trey found him before Lee and I did."

Joe went on. "Trey knew that Hershel saw the old chapel as a hideout. He'd probably been looking for him there ever since Hershel disappeared. He might not have been too worried about him being found alive. People wouldn't believe anything Hershel said."

The party broke up not too long after that. There were ramifications afterward, of course.

First, Meg left town that night, and as far as I know has never been seen in Warner Pier again. I now believe she told Trey she'd had an affair with Joe to make her husband jealous. That would be in line with the "tricky" philosophy she told me was the best way to deal with men.

She obviously knew about Trey's plan to build the snazzy resort hotel; I've always suspected he came up with the project because Meg wanted him to make some real money. But Trey denied she was involved in the murder and the murderous attacks on Joe and me, so she got away. If the Corbett family helped her or Trey, they didn't do it publicly.

As for her relationship with Joe when they were in high school, Joe asked me if I wanted to know more, and I declined. We've never mentioned Meg again, and I don't plan to bring her up. I hope I'm not as stupid as Trey.

Dolly Jolly came by TenHuis Chocolade a few days later and asked if the apartment over Aunt Nettie's shop would be available for rent the next fall.

"I don't usually rent it in the winter," Aunt Nettie said.

"I've decided to stay in Warner Pier year round!" Dolly said. "Living over a chocolate factory sure would smell good! Hope to find a job!"

"What kind of job are you interested in?"

"Food! Food-related!"

So that situation looks interesting.

A week after Trey was arrested a house painter named John Adolph called the county sheriff to report that someone had broken into his storage building and stolen his black Dodge panel truck. He'd been on vacation and had just missed it. Why, yes, he said, he had done several painting jobs for Trey Corbett's projects, and, yes, Trey was familiar with his workshop and knew where he stored his equipment. The panel truck turned up late the next October, after the leaves began to fall, in a ravine about a mile from Gray Gables. Fake numbers had been painted on its tag, with the zeros turned into eights.

As for Frank and Patsy, they're still together. If he's drinking and staying out nights, Greg Glossop hasn't spread the world yet.

Joe says he suspected that Frank had been mishandling Hershel's trust. When the final accounting was made the judge asked some pointed questions—or so Joe heard over at the courthouse. But in the end Frank wasn't accused of any misdeeds.

But all that was later. The big discussion between Joe and me came the night Trey was arrested. I'd stayed to lock the shop up after our little chocolate-coffee-brandy gathering. Joe stayed, too, because he'd left his boat at Gray Gables, and he needed a ride home.

As Mike went out the front door, he clapped Joe on the shoulder and said, "I am relieved to have this settled. Now we'll put our discussion item back on the workshop agenda. Ten a.m. Wednesday. City Hall."

Joe just nodded, but I stopped Mike. "What are you all conspicuous about? I mean, conspiring! What are you conspiring about?"

Mike grinned happily. "Lee, you're so funny!" Then he spoke to Joe. "I guess you keep her around for laughs, right?"

"Actually," Joe said, "she never does that when we're alone." Then Mike left, and I locked the front door.

While I was locking up I realized that Joe had spoken the truth. I rarely made my verbal gaffs when he and I were by ourselves. Why was that?

I didn't try to answer my own question. I wanted

to ask Joe about this "agenda item" Mike had mentioned. Joe had gone out the alley door and was standing between my van and our Dumpster.

I followed him out into the alley and locked the door. Then I demanded an explanation. "Joe, what are you and Mike up to?"

"Up to?"

"Don't act innocent. He's made several references to this mysterious 'agenda item,' and you even called him once and talked about it."

"Oh. That."

"Yes. That. What's going on?"

"Warner Pier has never had a city attorney. They just hire somebody if they need legal counsel. Now Mike's going to recommend that they put someone on retainer. Just part-time. I'm going to apply for the job. But Hershel's death put a crimp in our plans. They couldn't hire me if I was involved with a crime."

"But you said you never wanted to practice law again. You gave me all this stuff about the sanctity of craftsmanship and the morality of boat restoration."

Joe laughed. "I'm trying to have my craftsmanship and eat it, too. Warner Pier isn't exactly swamped with legal problems. I think I can read over the contracts and warn the city councillors that they're about to break the law without giving up Vintage Boats."

"I don't like that. You're already handling two full-time jobs—winding up the Ripley estate and the boat shop. Now you're going to take on another job part-time?"

"The problem with the two jobs I have now is that neither of them pays on a regular basis. The boats pay when you finish a job or when you sell a boat. The Ripley estate, as you know, doesn't pay at all, since I'm still determined not to take any money on that deal. Oh, I'm keeping track of my expenses—lunch, mileage, phone calls. But my real aim is to get the estate in good enough shape that I can give the Warner Point property to the city."

He tugged at my hand until I was facing him. "Don't tell anyone that, okay? Not even Mike. I may not be able to work it out, so I can't make a commitment."

"Did anybody ever tell you you're an awfully nice guy?"

"I'm a guy who feels guilty. The city should have had that property all along. In a way, I was responsible for Clementine's deciding to build a summer place here and snagging the property out from under Mike's nose. It's simply a matter of justice. But her estate is so far in debt I may not be able to bring it off. I've had one offer, and I may yet have to sell it. So please don't say anything."

I kissed him. He kissed me back. After a few moments of this, he spoke. Actually, he swore.

"Dammit! I went to a lot of trouble—moonlight boat rides, trips up the river for dinner—so we could have this conversation in a romantic setting. And we wind up having it leaning on a Dumpster!"

I laughed. "I don't see anything particularly romantic about your taking a third job. I barely fit into your schedule as it is."

"The point of the city job is really you."

"Why?"

"You've made me realize that I don't want to live in one room in the back of a boat shop for the rest of my life. I might even want to get married."

"Oh." I gulped.

"Or I might if I could interest the right person," Joe said.

"You probably could," I said. "But people who've made one bad decision are sometimes scared of making another."

"Are you scared?"

"I don't pull my malapropisms when we're alone. Maybe that means I feel safe. Are you scared?"

"Terrified. I'm scared of losing you." He kissed me again. "We don't have to rush into anything, but I don't want to wait forever."

"No," I said. "Not forever."

CHOCOLATE CHAT

DUTCHING LEADS TO CHOCOLATE BARS

- Dutch chocolate maker Coenraad Johannes van Houten revolutionized the drinking of chocolate. Van Houten invented what Americans call cocoa, patenting his process in 1826.

- Van Houten first used a hydraulic press to reduce the percentage of cacao fat in his product. The resulting powder was then treated with alkaline salts, a process known as "Dutching." This improves its ability to be mixed, though it does not make it dissolve more easily.

- Van Houten's new process meant the old thick beverage, which required frequent stirring, was now much easier to prepare and only needed to be stirred now and then. His process also meant that cocoa and chocolate could now be produced on a large scale. Chocolate was no longer the elite, expensive drink and food it had been.

- In 1847 the British firm of J S Fry & Sons developed a method of mixing cocoa powder, sugar, and melted cacao butter into a product that could be cast in a mold.

- The chocolate bar was born, and the taste buds of chocoholics have been grateful ever since.

About the Author

JoAnna Carl is the pseudonym for a multipublished mystery writer. She spent twenty-five years in the newspaper business, working as a reporter, a feature writer, an editor, and a columnist. She holds a degree in journalism from the University of Oklahoma and also studied in the O.U. Professional Writing program. She lives in Oklahoma but summers in Michigan, where the Chocoholic Mysteries are set. She has one daughter who works for a chocolate maker and another who is a CPA. She may be reached through her Web site, www.joannacarl.com.